☞ **W9-BZM-875**

moonglass

moonglass

Jessi Kirby

SIMON & SCHUSTER BFYR

NEW YORK LONDON TORONTO SYDNEY

For my family

SIMON & SCHUSTER BFYR
An imprint of Simon & Schuster Children's Publishing Division
1230 Avenue of the Americas, New York, New York 10020

For information about special discounts for bulk purchases, please contact Simon & Schuster Special Sales at 1-866-506-1949 or business@simonandschuster.com.
The Simon & Schuster Speakers Bureau can bring authors to your live event. For more information or to book an event, contact the Simon & Schuster Speakers Bureau at 1-866-248-3049 or visit our website at www.simonspeakers.com.
Book design by Krista Vossen.
The text for this book is set in Fairfield.
Manufactured in the United States of America
2 4 6 8 10 9 7 5 3 1
Library of Congress Cataloging-in-Publication Data
Kirby, Jessi.
Moonglass / Jessi Kirby.
p. cm.
Summary: At age seven, Anna watched her mother walk into the surf and drown, but nine years later, when she moves with her father to the beach where her parents fell in love, she joins the cross-country team, makes new friends, and faces her guilt.
ISBN 978-1-4424-1694-9 (hardcover)
[1. Beaches—Fiction. 2. Moving, Household—Fiction. 3. Fathers and daughters—Fiction. 4. Guilt—Fiction. 5. Suicide—Fiction. 6. California—Fiction.] I. Title.
PZ7.K633522Moo 2011
[Fic]—dc22
2010037389
ISBN 978-1-4424-1696-3 (eBook)

FIRST
EDITION

acknowledgments

I've always heard that in life we gravitate toward people who embody the qualities we most admire, and for me it's absolutely true. Especially when it comes to the people I've had the privilege to know and work with thus far.

First off are two women I couldn't respect or adore more: my agent, Leigh Feldman, who I've loved since the day we met for her honesty, integrity, and the witty kind of irreverence I've always wanted to have; and my editor, Alexandra Cooper, whose graceful and incisive hand is moved by a passionate enthusiasm that won my heart the very first time we spoke. I have so much gratitude for these two and their indispensible assistants, Eric Amling and Ariel Colletti. I would also like to thank Justin Chanda and the entire team at Simon & Schuster Books for Young Readers for making me feel like a member of the family from the very beginning. And I owe a very special thank-you to designer extraordinaire, Krista Vossen, whose cover still makes me smile giddily.

On the writing end, I wouldn't have a book without two stellar critique partners I'm lucky enough to read with and learn from: Jonathan Stephens and Kirsten Rice. The two of you have taught me more than you know or I can even put into words. Here's to many more exchanges of drafts and ideas, encouragement, and honest opinions. Speaking of honest opinions, I cannot forget the very first person to read the entire manuscript (as I wrote it!), and give me hers: Carol Abifadel, who happens to be kind of a genius and one of my very dear friends.

Most importantly, I owe a love-filled thank-you to my friends and family who cheered me on and believed in me when I said this was what I wanted to do. Especially my husband, Schuyler, who never ceases to amaze me with the depth of his patience, generosity of his heart, and knack for helping me out with my dialogue.

I am a lucky girl to have you all, and not a day goes by that I don't remember that.

I read once that water is a symbol for emotions. And for a while now I've thought maybe my mother drowned in both.

I watch as the wind whips long blond hair around her face. Whitecaps glimmer in the lights from the pier. She doesn't flinch as the cold hits her. She's numb from feeling too much, and she has shut it all out. Her eyes are focused on an invisible horizon, and she walks straight out. The waves slap at her, plastering her gauzy skirt to her legs. She's in up to her chest, and now, as the water surges, she breathes in sharply, involuntarily, because of the cold.

Her mind is clear at this moment. Nothing but the purity of the cold and the possibility of total peace. She bends her knees and lets the water hit her chin, takes some of the bitter saltiness into her mouth, then lets it run out, eyes still focused on the beyond. She doesn't take a breath before going under, but exhales completely and dissolves into the blackness without thinking about anything.

Not even me.

1

Rain and wind pelted the ocean's surface so hard it looked like it was boiling. In the passenger seat of our VW bus, I shivered despite the warm, muggy air. My dad jumped into the driver's seat and shook the rain off.

"Weird summer storm, huh?" Water dripped from his face as he tried to catch my eye.

I looked away.

"You ready? Sure you've got everything?"

"Yep. Got it all." I paused, staring straight out the windshield. "Oh, wait—except for my friends, my school, my life . . ."

"Anna—"

"I know. I'm gonna love it there. It'll be just *great*."

He started to say something but shook his head instead, cranked the key, and turned the music up to a volume that made it clear we were finished talking. I felt a pang of regret for being like that with him, but kept my eyes on the beach that he'd decided, without even asking me, to leave. The beach where I'd found a simple peace on my morning runs, and trolled for boys with my friends on lazy summer afternoons, and where I'd caught my last waves of the day, just as the sun slipped into the ocean. It was where my life was.

And where my mother had left hers.

I couldn't understand it any more than I could put it into words, but tangled up with my anger at my dad over moving was a sense of guilt that ran deep in me. The stretch of water here belonged to my mother. And, somehow, leaving felt horribly wrong.

I would never have said it, though, even if I thought it'd change his mind. I knew well the boundaries we'd drawn. Instead I rested my temple on the rain-cooled passenger window and watched the churning ocean disappear through a blur of gray.

The dark all around threw me off. Apparently I had actually fallen asleep while *pretending* to be asleep so as to avoid talking to my dad. He put the car in park and stepped out to open the locked gate in front of us. When he looked back and motioned for me to slide over to the driver's seat, I did so grudgingly and pulled our old bus forward, far enough so he had to back up a step or two, just to see if I could make him move. He didn't seem to notice.

"You wanna drive on down, Anna?"

It was a stab at peace. Every time we'd talked for the last few weeks, we'd argued about why I couldn't just live with my grandma and finish out high school at home, in Pismo Beach. Either he didn't get it or he didn't care how unfair it was, the way he'd changed everything like it was nothing. In a week's time he'd taken a promotion and a transfer, packed up our life, and come to the cove to start a new one. Just like that.

His generous concession was that I could stay with my grandma for the rest of the summer. So while he'd moved in and started work, I'd spent my days on the beach, trying to feel the normal fun and lightness of summer. Shelby and Laura and I went on with our summer traditions. We paddled out at the pier on the Fourth of July so we could watch the fireworks fall down like rain over our heads. We camped out on the dunes, feasting on s'mores and getting spinney on wine coolers. We snuck into the hotel pools only to be shooed out by the owners, who'd known us since forever. And we didn't mention that I was leaving. Instead we laughed at tourist boys for their loud board shorts and backward wet suits, and then at ourselves for flirting with them anyway.

But none of it was the same. For me, everything we did was weighted with the knowledge that I was leaving and the stark realization that their lives would go on nearly the same without me once I was gone. Mine was the one that would change.

It was a lonely thought, and I tried not to think about it. I had other worries. As soon as my dad had made his decision to take the transfer, something in him had shifted. There was a distance between us that was more than the result of me being angry about moving. He was just *off* somehow, only half there, and it unsettled me the same way watching a storm move in over the water did. I could tell he was trying hard to hide it and somehow hold on to the careful balance it had taken us so long to build. But the moment he'd made the decision to leave, that balance was all off. Which brought us to the cove.

"No, I don't wanna drive down." I scooted back over to my

seat, and he got in, probably resigned to the fact that I was going to draw this out.

"Suit yourself." He sounded tired. I looked out my window, arms crossed, and he tried again. "I think when you see the place you may have a change of heart."

When I didn't respond, he sighed and put the bus in gear. We rolled down a steep hill past a carved wooden sign that read CRYSTAL COVE STATE PARK. Just beyond it the road turned to dirt. He perked up and pointed out his open window to a tiny yellow cottage.

"This was the first building here, Building One. It was the check-in site for the old tent campers." He said it like he was conducting a tour.

"Hm." I curled my toes around the crank on the door and pushed it to crack the window. Cool salt air flowed in, and my mood lightened a little. We were definitely close to the water. The crash of the next wave confirmed it. I breathed in deeply, and my dad glanced over at me just before I could hide a small involuntary smile. He didn't bother to hide his own as we trundled slowly across a white wooden bridge, our tires *thunk-thunk*ing over each plank.

The road made a little curve and opened up to a view that humbled me. A yellow moon hung low over calm, glassy water, creating a path of light that began at the horizon and ended with a splash on the slick sand. Just down the beach I could make out a point dotted with the silhouettes of jagged rocks, where a small wave stood up and broke with a surprisingly loud crash.

I rolled my window all the way down, and my dad broke into a grin. "This"—he motioned with his hand—"is our new front yard." He waited for me to say something. "Not too bad, huh?"

In spite of myself I felt a little ripple of optimism rising. I looked at the row of cottages illuminated by pale moonlight, and attempted to sound only mildly interested. "So . . . we actually get to live here? *In* the park?" He nodded, obviously proud. "Which one is ours?"

He took his foot off the gas, and our tires crunched over the dirt road. "It's right . . . up . . . here." We came to a stop in front of a small white cottage with blue trim. Our new home. Literally *on* the beach. "Not bad for employee housing, huh?"

My resolve to stay mad was slipping away. Fast. I didn't fight the genuine smile I felt spreading across my face. "Not bad."

He got out and stood, arms stretched above his head, smiling out at the ocean. "Wanna jump in?" A wave broke, then rushed up the sand like an answer to his invitation.

"Seriously?"

"Yeah. That drive was brutal without the A/C."

I shook my head, knowing that once I got into the water, my hard-fought battle would lose its bluster. He knew it too, and more often than not had coaxed me into a surf or a swim together to diffuse a fight. I watched for a second, torn a little between not wanting to concede and the desire to let the day's tension slip beneath the slick surface of the water. I could swim straight out into the shining path of moonlight and let it go for now. Give it a chance. By the time I reached into my backpack to grab a bathing suit, my dad had already made his way to the water with steps so light they made me wonder if I'd been wrong about the change I'd sensed in him.

The water was warmer than I'd expected. I waded out, enjoying the slap of white water against my legs. When a wave rose in front of me, I took a breath and dove under. The familiar surge passed over me, bringing a calm kind of happiness, and I surfaced to meet the cool, fresh smell of the beach at night. Some things were the same everywhere.

I turned to float on my back and take the place in. Down on the beach it looked like a snapshot from long ago. Our beat-up VW bus parked in front of the weathered beach cottage was perfect. A simple, dreamy beach life. Sort of. Despite the calm that was all around me, I found myself almost waiting for the first ripples of the past to appear. I'd known the name Crystal Cove long before my dad had told me we were moving. According to my grandma, it was where my parents had met so many years ago, on summer vacation. My mother had been here, before I was even a thought. Maybe walked the beach, watched the sunset, went for a night swim . . .

My dad popped up behind me. "Almost too good to be true, huh?" His smile made him look like a kid.

I felt a momentary softness. It really was amazing, and he really was trying. Hard. "Yeah, it's pretty great."

"It is." He said it almost to himself, then was quiet a long moment, and I knew what he was thinking. What he had to be thinking. I tensed and willed him not to feel the need to bring it up.

"This is where your mom and I first met, you know. Right down there on the beach." He pointed south, suddenly wistful, and I froze. Though I'd known, hearing him say it turned my stomach.

"Yeah. I know." I took a breath and went under, pulling myself past him beneath the surface. I didn't want to go down this path tonight. Actually, I wasn't sure I wanted to go down this path ever. We didn't talk about these things. Our comfortable, mostly easy way of getting along with each other depended on *not* bringing up my mom. And now here we were. Amidst a whole lot of history I didn't want to dig up.

I surfaced a few feet away and tried to sound light, but there was an edge to my voice. "Sooo, are we gonna stay out here all night, or do I get to see the place?"

My dad glanced down the beach, started to say something, and then thought better of it. "Yeah. Let's go." With that he looked over his shoulder just in time to catch the next wave in. I waited for another one and pushed off the sand with my toes. The swell lifted me, and I put my arms out in the face of it, gaining speed all the way to the sand.

As I stood, twisting water out of my hair, my dad strode over the sand below the dirt road in front of our house. I heard a tiny click, and a motion detector light flipped on. When it did, I noticed for the first time what looked like a condemned cottage sitting on the beach, backed up to the cliff. A drooping fence surrounded it, overgrown with ice plant, setting it apart from our row of restored cottages on the hill. I hadn't even realized it was there. Now, though, in the yellow light, it stood like a piece of history preserved in time. The cracked windows were barely translucent from the mist and sand accumulated on them, and the whole shack leaned precariously, as if the weight of the vines sprawled over it were too much for it to bear. I shivered a little.

"Anna, you coming?" My dad reached into the bus and grabbed two towels, wrapping one around his waist. He didn't even glance over at the dilapidated cottage. "Here. Towel for ya." He held the other one out to me.

I fumbled with it for a second, then slung it over my shoulder, still unable to look away from the cottage. As we picked our way up the uneven stepping stones in front of our new house,

I opened my mouth to ask about it, but changed my mind just as the light clicked off. I paused and squinted at the cottage in the dark, waiting for something. But there was nothing. Just the crash of another wave and the stillness that followed.

My dad put the key into the dead bolt and nudged the door with his shoulder. We stepped into hot, stale air and darkness. The smell was unfamiliar but not unpleasant—something of the old wood the cottage was built of. The light flipped on, and he went straight to opening the windows.

"Gets a little stuffy in here all closed up." He pulled a latch and threw open another window.

In the dim light I could see that the hardwood floor had been painted over with brick red paint. The pale yellow walls were smudged and cracked. It wasn't my grandmother's house, that was for sure. Once my dad had gotten here, he'd called to say it probably was a good idea for me to stay back with her while he came down here to get settled. I could see why. The place wasn't exactly homey. Not much hung on the walls or softened the emptiness of it. In the few weeks I'd spent with my grand-mother, I had grown accustomed to a comfortable life. She doted on me like I pictured her doting on my dad as a kid, complete with a commercial-perfect breakfast every morning and clean sheets every Sunday. Here I could see that wouldn't be the case.

He must have seen it on my face. "I know. It needs some help. We'll have plenty of time for that. I've been putting in a lot of hours since I got here." I nodded skeptically, eyeing his sunburned face. "Plus, I figured maybe you'd have fun deco-rating." I was silent. "Hey. I got started." He gestured to a set of shelves in a little alcove.

In his own way he *had* tried. Scattered over the shelves were pictures of us that I knew were his favorites. Almost all were images of us smiling at the camera from a boat or our surfboards, happy and tanned. Between the picture frames were a few seashells—his attempt at decorating. I set my bag down.

"As long as you're forcing me to be here, I guess there are a few things I could do with the place." I gestured at the giant picture window framing the moon and the water. "I don't think we should put curtains up there. It's too pretty to cover up." We looked out at the water, quiet, and it felt like one of those moments that was heavy with the things we didn't want to say out loud.

"Well, come on. I'll give you the full tour." He put a hand on my shoulder and steered me through a narrow doorway, then flipped another light switch. "This"—he swept his arm over a bare room with a bed in the middle—"is my room."

"Wow, Dad . . . this is depressing." I glanced around. On his ancient dresser was a plate-size abalone shell he had found on a dive in Mexico. Another attempt at decorating. Above it hung a black-and-white picture of my mom, from when they had first met. At this beach. In it she stood at the waterline looking down, like she was unaware of the camera. She wore a white sundress and a calm almost-smile. I squinted to see if I could glimpse any of the cottages in the background, but then felt my dad looking at it too, starting to get lost in the thought of it again.

I clapped my hands together and looked around. "So. Where's my room?"

"Well, you have to go through my room to get to yours, but you have an outside door too." My mind hummed at the potential of this as I followed him past his bed and to another doorway. He stopped, hand on the doorknob to my room, and turned abruptly to face me, so that I almost ran into him.

"Listen." He took me by the shoulders. "I know I asked a lot of you, to pick up and move."

My eyes welled up instantly, for too many reasons to name.

"And maybe you don't understand all the reasons I decided to take the transfer." *Maybe* I didn't understand?

I kept myself from saying anything, because I knew exactly how it would come out. I was too tired to start it all over again, so I let him go on.

"Honestly, I'm not sure I do either. But I think, if you give it a chance, you're gonna love it here. It's a pretty special place. Wait till you wake up in the morning and look outside." He squeezed my shoulders, searched my eyes for an answer.

I sniffed and nodded, trying to smooth it over for now. It couldn't be easy for him, either. "That beach out there is the only thing you have going for your case, you know."

He smiled and opened the door to my room. All of my furniture was there, unpacked. He had even made up the bed.

"You arrange it however you want. I just didn't want you to come home to an empty room." He cleared his throat. "Most of your stuff is still in those boxes, but I got a few things out. You still have plenty of time to get settled in before school starts."

I stood in the middle of my new room, amidst my things, and tried to feel it. The word "home." But it wasn't there yet. For me, anyway. When my dad said it, though, it had a ring of old familiarity to it, and that was somehow comforting. I sat down on the edge of my bed, which felt the same as it had back home, ran my hand over the same worn-soft quilt.

He rubbed his neck. "I gotta open the park in the morning, so I won't be here when you get up, but I'll leave some money

on the counter if you wanna walk up to the Shake Shack for
lunch. We can go for a dive or a surf or something when I get
off." He walked over and kissed the top of my head. "Good
night, kiddo. I love you."

"Mm-hm. You too."

When the door closed, I stood up and looked around again.
On top of my dresser sat my jar of sea glass, full with the
greens and blues of countless hours spent combing the beach.
I walked over and examined it, wondering what the ocean
might uncover here, on this beach. Maybe a rare piece—purple, or yellow, or red. I set the jar on my nightstand, where it
belonged, then changed out of my wet swimsuit.

Any other day I would have opened my door to the outside
and sat on the step, breathing in the night and listening to the
ocean. But this day had been long and heavy, and the only thing
I wanted was to start over in the light of the morning. I climbed
into the cool of my sheets and switched off the light. For a
long time I lay there listening to the sounds of my new home.
The most noticeable was the rhythmic smack of waves on the
shore, and then the static-like sound of their foam rolling up in
disorganized ripples. The rest of the night outside was silent.

I wondered what Laura and Shelby were doing at this moment.
Thought of my grandma, probably sitting up with her glass of
wine and a "late movie," like she loved to watch. I replayed the
conversation I'd had with my dad, spoken and unspoken, until
I had myself convinced we'd be all right here . . . somehow. But
then I rolled onto my side and thought of my mother, here on
this beach.

And like a reflex I closed my eyes against it all.

2

I needed to run. Because for as long as I could remember, it was the one time when I could just move and not think of *anything*. Being in the water could calm me, but it wasn't the same. When I was younger, after my mom was gone, the ocean was the place I went to be near her, where I would dive under the waves, thinking I'd maybe catch a glimpse of her there, hair splayed out like a mermaid's—swimming, beautiful and strong and free. She felt close and peaceful that way, and since then, the water had become the place where I felt most at home. But being here, where she'd been before I even existed, where she and my dad had a history he had laid to rest until the night before, it somehow all felt too close. So I needed to run.

I walked the narrow path to the sand and glanced at the run-down beach cottage as I passed it. In the weak morning light it seemed especially still and quiet. All the windows on the first story were hidden under sprawling bougainvillea, but upstairs I could make out a small window shrouded in dirt, and a tiny sagging balcony facing the water. Someone had woken up to a deserted beach a long, long time ago and had probably seen the same simple beauty of pelicans gliding in a line, wing tips hovering impossibly close to the surface of the swells.

The beach and its cottages stood out in stark contrast to the other side of Pacific Coast Highway. Across four lanes, lining the hills was a series of homes that were really more like the celebrity compounds I'd seen in magazines. The higher up the hill they were, the taller the columns and the wider the arches got, like each house was in competition with the next. It was ridiculous. And sort of intimidating, if I was being honest with myself.

These were the people whose kids I was gonna go to school with. Kids who sat up there on the hill with million-dollar views of the ocean, but who probably never really *saw* it. They probably liked the status it gave them, to live near the beach. But other than that, I guessed it was just a pretty backdrop for their BMWs and designer clothes.

As soon as I had the thought, a tiny part of me realized how self-righteous that would sound if I actually said it out loud. But still. My friends and I prided ourselves on cute thrift store finds and our ability to dig up change anytime we needed to put gas into our old cars. Those were the things that entertained us and made life fun. And now they were the things that were missing. Before I let myself think about it too much, I walked over the sand and breathed in the morning.

At the waterline I looked south to where my dad had pointed the night before, and I shook out my legs before starting off in a slow jog. On a good day mine were the first footprints on the sand and I floated, legs moving effortlessly over a landscape of sand, shells, and seaweed. Today my legs felt a little tight, so I eased into it. As I ran, my eyes automatically went to the ground, scanning for sea glass. It was an old habit. One that probably slowed me down. I followed the high tide line and the bits of shells, seaweed, and pebbles, but nothing glimmered at me from the sand, so I let my eyes wander up and over the waves that broke gray-green in the rising sun. Down the beach, in the shadow of the cliff, two heads bobbed in the water. A wave rose behind them, and one of the surfers paddled hard to catch it. I stretched out my strides and settled into a smoother pace, curious about the guys in the water.

As I got closer, I could see they were shortboarders and that they were sitting practically on the rocks, waiting for a set to come through. A look at the flat glassy water said they were either extremely optimistic or extremely inexperienced. I decided they were good-looking, charming optimists and picked up my speed a little more. The sun had emerged from the morning gray, and the warmth of it loosened me up. As I neared the point, a small wave rose off it, and both surfers paddled hard. One stood and pumped his tiny surfboard with his legs, trying to maintain some kind of momentum. My dad would have rolled his eyes. He surfed a ten-foot single fin board and never wore a leash. Had he caught the same wave, he would have paddled in smoothly, popped up, and gone straight to the nose to finish out the ride.

I hopped over their backpacks and turned my attention to the point, where black cliffs rose sharply from the green water and mussel-covered rocks. Briefly I let myself wonder how my parents had met here. I couldn't even picture them that young.

Was it my dad out in the water and my mom walking the beach early in the morning? He'd probably tell me if I asked. He'd probably be happy to.

I dismissed the thought almost as quickly as it had come into my head, and hopped over a tangled-up strand of seaweed. Three more paces brought me to a large rock, and I tagged it with one foot, pushed off, and turned around. As I did, I stole a sideways glance at the guys in the water, which wasn't enough to tell how old they were or what they looked like, but enough to know that they were looking in my direction, probably trying to figure out those same things. I put my head down, suddenly self-conscious, and picked it up again. This time to a pace that was faster than comfortable. A slow burn spread out in my chest as I flew over the sand, hoping they didn't realize.

Thankfully, just up the beach something caught my eye in the brightening sunlight. It looked like a piece of frosty ice sitting on the sand. Out of place, but next to invisible if you weren't looking for it. I stopped abruptly to pick up the thick half-dollar-size piece of sea glass, then turned it in my fingers and held it up to the light. It was pitted and translucent on the outside, but there was one edge that was still crystal clear, a window to the inside of the glass. In the center I saw the small spots my mom had told me about. Something about the process of making the glass that meant it was close to a hundred years old. She would have said it wasn't a great piece, because of the broken edge.

I liked the ones with the chips in them, though, where you could see what the piece looked like bare and pure, before the ocean had tumbled it around and worn it down. The beauty of a piece like this was that after it had been worn down, something had happened to crack it open. Something big.

I curled my fingers around it and ran the rest of the way back, switching it from hand to hand and feeling like I had found a small treasure.

By the time I stood stretching in the sand, the beach was alive and the sun shone brightly as families lugging umbrellas and sand toys staked out their spots. The unmistakable smells of syrup, coffee, and bacon wafted over, drawing me up the beach to where I could see small groups of people milling about. Out in front of what must have at one time been another cottage, a sign read THE BEACHCOMBER. The deck was packed, and the sounds of clinking plates and happy Sunday morning chatter almost drowned out the waves. The people waiting stood by in sunglasses, smiling and laughing while their kids played happily in the sand. It was definitely a different set of people from what I was used to seeing up north, and it was exactly what I'd expected here. The people dressed to impress, even for breakfast at the beach, which made me feel distinctly out of place in my sweaty shorts and sports bra. Actually, I would have felt out of place in this crowd no matter how I was dressed. I watched a moment longer before turning to head for a shower.

"So. Do you always run that fast?" a voice behind me asked. I turned around and saw a tiny blond girl in a long sundress, heeled sandals, and sunglasses the size of her face. She shifted the giant bag on her shoulder, and a fluffy white dog poked its head out.

I glanced around. Nobody else she could be talking to. "Uh, no, not always. Why?" I couldn't decide if I was suspicious or annoyed.

"Well, I never ran, because I always heard it shortens your muscles, but I was watching the Olympics this summer, and all of the runner girls are really skinny, but not too muscley, kind of like you, and so I decided to do cross-country this year. You know, running on a team." She blinked a few times, waited for a response, then clarified, "To lose some weight."

I looked at her tiny, perfectly tanned frame, trying to figure out if she was serious. She didn't seem to notice, and I let her go right on with it.

"Anyway, it starts tomorrow, and so I told my dad that this would have to be our last breakfast down here, because the only thing I like to order is the macadamia pancakes, and they're *totally* fatty."

I had to say something. Anything. "Huh. I don't think I could swear off pancakes." Lame, but what did she want me to say? Tell her that she clearly didn't need to diet? That lugging that bag around with her dog in it was probably workout enough for her skinny arms?

She looked me over, then smiled sweetly. "Well, could you imagine what you would look like if you ran *and* watched what you ate? My mom is, like, the queen of working out *and* dieting, and she hasn't even had to have lipo yet or anything. Well, besides Botox, but she's almost *forty-five*. Can you imagine?" She smiled, clearly proud, and a little breathless. I pursed my lips together, hard, trying not to smile. She was actually serious. She went on. "So are you here on vacation or something?"

"Actually, I just moved here. Last night."

She stuck out her tiny French-manicured hand. "I'm Ashley Whitmore. I would have been the sixth if I was a boy."

I shook her hand and was surprised that she had a good, firm handshake. I half-expected her to curtsy or something.

"I'm Anna. Ryan." We stood for a moment, looking out toward the water, and I felt totally justified in my earlier assumptions about the people I'd be going to school with. I wished Shelby and Laura could meet this girl, just to see that people like her really existed. Maybe I'd call them later.

I turned south to hide my smile, and something caught my eye. It was a man, and he was . . . *crawling?* I shaded my eyes and squinted down the beach at him, trying to make sense of it or see if I was wrong. I wasn't. He was an old man, bear-crawling on the tips of his fingers and toes toward us. I watched, waiting for him to stand up or sit down or something, but he just kept . . . crawling. Ashley sidled up to me with an easy friendliness that made me feel a little guilty.

"So. Where are you going to school?" Only half-listening, I squinted at something that swung back and forth from the man's neck.

"Oh, um, I'm going to Coast High." As he crawled closer, I could make out several things hanging from his neck. I could also see that he had his ankles wrapped in white tape that stood out against his taught, thin legs. Ashley put her hand on my shoulder and squeezed.

"*Serious?* That's where I'm going! I'm transferring from private school because my parents say I need a bigger taste of the 'real world.'" She chewed her gum thoughtfully, and I wondered how "real" Coast High, in the richest part of Orange County, could actually be. "I don't really mind, because I *hated* our uniforms. And the girls there could be kind of catty." I caught a whiff of watermelon as she turned to me, cracking her gum. "We should maybe stick together—so we're not, like, alone at first. I don't know anybody who goes there." She took a breath, and I could see that a new thought had come into her head. "Hey! Why don't you run on the cross-country team with me? It could help us both out."

I looked at her. "What do you mean?"

"Well, you know, you're all athletic and pretty in a strong sort of way. You kind of have a surfer-girl thing going for you, with your brown skin and the wavy blond hair and all. If you join with me, you could help me run fast, and I could help you diet and totally perfect how pretty you already are!"

I'd been watching the crawling man approaching the sand in front of us, but now three of the four things she'd said processed, and simultaneously I wondered if I needed to diet and whether or not she had ever been punched. Then I wondered if she was this friendly with everyone. She was smiling, like she'd thought up the greatest idea ever.

I cleared my throat, stalling for an answer she wouldn't be able to argue with. "Um . . . I usually just like to run by myself. And I think I'll be fine without a diet. Besides, don't you think junior year is a little late to start a new sport?" The crawling man was directly in front of us, and I could now see that the things hanging from his neck were crosses of different sizes. They swung heavily, making his unnatural crawl look even more painful. *What in the world?* People here were turning out to be all kinds of crazy.

Ashley breezed on. "Oh, I don't care about doing good in the races or anything. Besides, you looked fast. And if you're starting out in a new place, at least you'd have something to be, so you don't end up just lost in the crowd, because there's *nothing* worse than being alone while everyone else is part of something." She moved her hand from my shoulder down to my arm and squeezed again. "Come on, Anna. It'll be fun."

I decided I was entertained by Ashley. My friends and I were nice people, but I didn't think any of us would have befriended a perfect stranger so breezily. And with such seemingly good intentions that came out so, so wrong.

It was strange, but also kind of nice, considering. She did have a point about the lost-in-the-crowd thing. I had a feeling she probably made friends with people pretty easily, and that could be a good thing for me too, since I'd always been a little on the reserved side. She probably had offended a lot of people too, but maybe they all just overlooked it, as I was finding it surprisingly easy to do. She seemed genuinely oblivious to the fact that anything she said could be potentially insulting, and for some reason that made it kind of forgivable.

"Maybe I will," I said, already resigned to what I was about to say. "Join the team, I mean." She squealed and hugged me, which again seemed strange and not, at the same time. As she started to lay out a plan for what it would be good to wear to the first morning practice, the crawling man passed us, and I saw on his sweat-soaked T-shirt a single word. REPENT. Ashley interrupted herself midsentence.

"Isn't he sad? He does that every Sunday. Everyone calls him 'the Crystal Crawler.' My dad thinks he's just some old crazy, but I think he must feel really bad about something and he's doing his punishment, or repenitance, or whatever."

"You mean 'penance'?"

"I guess. I don't know. I'm not Catholic." We both watched as he crawled slowly on, seemingly oblivious to the kids darting in and out of the water in front of him. His calves were balled up tight, and the muscles shook with the effort of each step. I wanted someone to go take his arm and help him up.

"How far does he crawl?"

"I think he does the whole beach. He does it all day. Usually, after breakfast on Sundays, my dad goes back home to work and I stay down here awhile. I was here all day last weekend, and I saw him go by three times." She looked at her watch. "Anyway, we're supposed to meet at school tomorrow at seven thirty for our first practice. I've already met the coach. Do you have a ride?"

"Tomorrow?" I hadn't expected to have to subject myself to her perkiness so soon. I wasn't even sure I'd actually agreed. Ashley was looking at me expectantly. "Yeah, I guess." I watched the hunched figure for one more long moment, then turned back to her, resigned. "I'll be there."

"Good." She smiled. Her phone rang. "Oh, hang on a sec." She rummaged in her bag, around her little dog, like he was just another item in there. He didn't seem to mind. She pulled out a bright pink phone with a crystal-encrusted *A* on it, and I almost laughed out loud. *Of course.* "You're already there? Yeah, okay, I'll be right up. I'm coming right now. . . . I'm walking up there. The air is on, right? It's getting hot. Okay. *Okay.* Bye." She tucked the phone back into her purse and smiled.

"Someone picking you up?" I asked.

"Yeah. I gotta go, but I'll see you bright and early tomorrow, Anna. And don't eat breakfast before we run. That way your body will burn whatever you eat today, you know?"

I pressed my lips together to keep from laughing, then forced a bright sunshiny smile to match hers. "Thanks. I'll try to remember that."

She smiled and gave her shoulders a quick shrug. "No prob." With that she turned and made her way through the sand to the trail, surprisingly quick for a girl in heels. When she got to it, she stopped and reached down to dig some sand out from her shoe, then waved happily. "See ya!"

I waved back, then turned once again to go home. This had to be a joke. And now I was joining the cross-country team? Possibly a whole bunch of Ashleys? *Tomorrow?* So much for settling in.

I kicked a rock and watched as it bumped over the wet sand, coming to rest just as the Crystal Crawler put his hand beside it. He looked up, and our eyes met. His didn't look crazy at all. They were stark blue and somber. And resolved.

For a brief second I thought about kneeling down next to him. To ask what he felt so bad about.

Instead I offered a quick apology and walked a little faster.

3

I had just settled myself comfortably on my beach towel, sun soaking into my back, the smell of sunscreen drifting by, when the low hum of an engine got my attention. I lifted my head just enough to see a lifeguard unit approaching, a dark-haired young-ish guy at the wheel. As it passed, I smiled from behind my sun-glasses. The guard nodded his head, smiled back like you would at a waving toddler, and kept driving. Vaguely disappointed, I lay my head back down. He had probably been "warned" by my dad. I wouldn't have put it past my dad to give all the seasonal guards pictures of me and then make them sign a contract say-ing that they would refrain from any sort of interaction with the supervisor's daughter. I figured that one of these days that might actually work in my favor—the whole forbidden thing. So far, though, it hadn't really panned out. Back at home they had all been too scared of him, which struck me as funny. Of course he had to be different at work, but I couldn't picture him being scary. Distant, yes. But not scary.

I went back to feigning sleep but watched through my sunglasses as a pair of guys, definitely younger than me, tossed a football back and forth. Almost imperceptibly they tromped nearer and nearer with it. I knew this game and was annoyed that in a minute that football would "accidentally" come sailing in my direction. I sat up and scanned for older, better-looking options. Problem was, not many guys went to the beach just to sit around. Not the kind I was interested in, anyway. The tourist boys who came over from the inland wearing white puka shell necklaces did, but I viewed them with a disdain that bordered on contempt. They were the football throwers. The ones I wanted sat out in the water atop surfboards. Or in lifeguard towers.

There was one just to the north of me, too far away for me to see any detail, but the guard who stood in it looked like he was young. The fact that he stood the entire time meant he was probably in his first year. I watched as he scanned the water with his binoculars. He stopped abruptly at a point in my direction but beyond me, then set his binoculars down, grabbed his buoy, and hopped down into the pile of sand at the base of his tower.

I turned my attention to where he was running. Two kids had picked their way out onto the rocks, just south of where I sat. I looked out to the water beyond them but didn't see any waves coming in. The lifeguard sprinted past me, and I could see he was young, close to my age. And good-looking. And pissed off. When he got to the rocks, he put his hands to his mouth and yelled something at the boys, who didn't notice. I couldn't see any danger to them really, but he bounded over the rocks like he could do it in his sleep, and stopped right in front of them.

He didn't look like he was yelling, exactly, but he pointed out to the water, making a crashing motion with his arm and pointing to the rocks. The boys looked down at their feet, which had been outfitted in aqua socks by a concerned parent, and shrugged before making their way back over the rocks to the safety of the sand. The lifeguard jogged ahead of them, and looked back once before making his way to his tower.

On his way back he came close enough for me to notice the waves in the back of his brown hair and the freckles that dotted his tan shoulders. I wondered what color his eyes were, but he didn't so much as glance in my direction. So much for what I considered *my* two aces—blond hair and a bikini. Instant karma for being so bitchy about the football throwers.

I watched as he climbed back up the ladder to his tower and once again stood at his post. He picked up his binoculars and again pointed them at the rocks. It was definitely possible that I fell into the magnified circles of vision somewhere, which I found unnerving and intriguing at the same time. I pulled my hair back and twisted it up on top of my head before lying back. I bent one leg and flattened out my stomach. Then I pointed my chin at the sun, stuck out my chest the slightest bit, and tried to pretend he didn't exist.

I let the sun warm my skin, and my mind drifted with the sound of the waves. The sound was the same as it was back home, but the air was warmer here. And so far, it was better than I had thought it would be. There on the sand, the worries I'd had about coming and what it might dredge up felt far off and irrational. My house was on the beach, I'd sort of made a friend, and the lifeguards were cute. It was almost like a fresh start. Maybe that was what my dad was trying to do, in some strange way—give us a place to move on.

For the past couple of months, when he would drive up to my grandmother's on the weekend, he would show up tired and . . . depressed? I had assumed it was because it bothered him to be back where he and my mom had some history. Too many memories. Which was why it didn't make sense to me that he had taken the transfer in the first place. It was also what set me on edge about the whole thing. It never occurred to me that maybe it was the other way around. Maybe it was good for him to get away and look at a different stretch of ocean, one that didn't hold within it the sharpness of her absence.

Lying there under the sun, with the sand formed to cradle my body, I couldn't decide how I felt about that, exactly. The prospect of being somewhere different, where my mother had once been, still left me uneasy. At home I could avoid the places that made me think too much, could be sure that I didn't run into any unwanted memories. I could stay away from the places we had walked together, happy, and the places that held other, less sunny memories. Or if I ever chose, I could go to them, maybe even graze the same grains of sand with my bare feet. Here I didn't have a choice. I didn't know how to think of her here. Even if I wanted to know more, it had been so long since I'd asked anything, I wasn't sure I knew how to anymore.

I sat up and glanced at the lifeguard tower. He was still there, though now he leaned forward against the railing under the sun, looking straight out at the sparkling water. All up and down the sand, beachgoers splashed in the crystal blue. Kids on bodyboards kicked for waves that rolled under them without breaking. A couple floated out beyond the swim buoys, entangled, kissing the salt water from each other's faces.

I set my sunglasses down on my towel and walked down to the water's edge. Just like the night before, it was warmer than I'd expected. There was no tensing up, no breath holding when I got in. I dove under a little roller and swam underwater, eyes open. The clarity beneath the surface was shocking. On the bottom I could see the ripples made by the waves. I kicked down into the muted blue and scooped sand between my two hands, then let it flow out and settle back into a tiny pile. Almost out of air, I floated to the surface and burst through, happy. From where I floated I could see the lifeguard looking at the tide pools through his binoculars again. He must have been new, to be that worried about people on those rocks on a day like this. He was so focused on that spot, he probably didn't notice anything else.

I made my way back to the waterline and shook the water out of my hair, then walked toward the rocks. The tide had gone out, leaving the huge clusters exposed and shining. In every indentation there was water—crystal clear and warm. I picked my way over the rocks and peered into a pool that was small but deep. The tiny waving arms of sea anemones lined the sides all the way down to the bottom, which lay beneath smooth round pebbles. As I squinted into the pool, a drop of water made its way down my face, then landed silently in the water, becoming the center of a ring of ripples that radiated outward.

"Hey!" A voice behind me yelled. I paused and composed myself before standing up slowly. "Hey," he said, softening a little. "You shouldn't be out here this far. People get knocked over all the time, and then I gotta patch up all their cuts too, so why don't you come on in?" Out of breath, he extended his hand.

I smiled casually out at the flat ocean. "I think I'll be all right."

He put his sunglasses on top of his head, and I saw that his eyes were clear blue. They flashed frustration. "Listen. You need to come in." He looked over his shoulder, and I followed his gaze to the lifeguard truck I had seen earlier. "Now." He offered his hand again.

The truck slowed, then almost sank to a stop on the sand, and the guard inside put his binoculars up to his eyes and pointed them at us. I raised an eyebrow. "Supervisor?"

He looked back impatiently. "Yeah. Kind of. Can you just come back to the beach?" He had to be close to my age. Definitely good-looking. I decided to go along, and put out my hand to let him guide me back over the rocks.

"Thanks," I said once we were back on the sand and the watchful eyes of the lifeguard in the truck were gone.

"No worries. Just don't go out there again. Or else I'm gonna be pissed off that I have to run down here and peel you off the rocks." He pointed at his tower fifty yards or so up the beach, then looked at me for a long moment. "I gotta get back up there, uh . . ."

"Anna. I'm Anna," I said, putting my hand out again.

"Tyler." He grabbed it firmly. "Stay off the rocks. Or wait until I'm off duty." He looked at his watch. "Listen, I get off in a half hour, and the tide's gonna go out farther. If you're still here, we can go check out whatever you were looking at. You staying here?" He motioned up at the cottages that lined the beach.

"Yeah. Actually, I am. Just got in last night. I'll probably be out here a little while longer."

"Okay, then." He turned and jogged back to his tower. "Maybe I'll see you when I get off."

I smiled to myself, wondering how long I could go without him finding out who I was. It could be fun to be off-limits after all.

4

I spent the next half hour watching the late-stayers on the beach. It was the kind of perfect golden summer afternoon when you could tell people just didn't want to leave, even though it was Sunday and most of them had to get back to the reality of their alarm clocks the next morning. A couple sat on a single towel nearby, tan legs mingled together. The girl absently scooped up handfuls of sand and let it sift through her fingers as she leaned over to whisper something into her boyfriend's ear. He laughed, then lay back and pulled her over him for a long kiss that felt a little too intense to be watching. A peppy trumpet came from the Beachcomber, where the staff was lined up, saluting a rising black flag with a martini glass on it. Everyone cheered and clinked their glasses, a small burst of excitement before only the sound of the waves and an occasional voice drifted over on the breeze.

Suddenly a tinny voice came from Tyler's tower. I looked up to see him holding a megaphone to his mouth. "Attention on the beach. Lifeguard service is now finished for the day. Please exit the water or swim at your own risk. Thank you, and enjoy your evening." With that he closed up his tower, climbed down, and headed my way. I turned my head in the other direction and pretended to check out the tide pools as he jogged over.

"Hey, you're still here." He sat down and pushed his sunglasses up into the perfect waves of brown hair, which I appreciated. Nothing worse than talking to your own reflection. I saw his eyes again and figured he must have seen his fair share of girls who were more than happy to be "rescued." They were a kind of silvery blue and lined with thick, long lashes. Lashes that would sell mascara to those same girls.

I leaned back on my elbows. "Well, I couldn't turn down a guided tour of the beach. Plus, it's perfect out here right now." We both looked out at the water that sparkled gold as the sun made its way toward the horizon.

He buried his toes in the sand. "So, you renting a cottage here with family?"

"Yeah. Well, just my dad."

"A little father-daughter trip? Nice." He looked around. "Where's he at?"

"He's around here somewhere. Actually, I haven't seen him all day, which is kinda funny. He's probably off on the other end of the beach somewhere, looking for shells."

"Huh. Good, because he told all of us to stay away from you."

I stopped abruptly. "What?"

"I'm kidding, I'm kidding. I've just seen it before. Most dads don't like their daughters hanging around with some guy they just met on the beach."

I laughed nervously and nodded. "Oh." Then silence. A seagull cried out behind us. I traced a figure eight in the sand.

"So. You wanna walk or something?" He grinned at me, and at that moment I would have thought anything he said sounded good. I tried to appear casual as I checked the beach for any sign of my dad.

"Sure."

We walked a few quiet paces, and I racked my brain for something to say. Nothing particularly witty or charming came to mind, so I settled on small talk. "So how long have you been a lifeguard here?"

He kicked a mussel shell out in front of us. "This is my second season."

I nodded, figuring he was seventeen or so. You could start lifeguarding at sixteen years old, something my dad had hassled me about doing this summer. "How do you like it?"

"It's a pretty killer job. Last summer kind of sucked, being a rookie. They do stupid shit—'scuse me, stupid stuff—to you, but it's that way everywhere. This year's better, except we have a new boss who's a total ass."

I cringed a little. "Really? What's his problem?" I wasn't sure if I wanted to know the answer, but I was morbidly curious at the same time.

"I don't know. He's totally old-school and worked here forever ago. He started out when he was, like, fifteen or something and worked his way up, so now that he's back, he cruises around like he knows everything." He stopped, checking to see if I was interested—which, of course, I was. "Anyway, it just sucks because none of us ever know when he's gonna come by and harp on us out of nowhere. He's just a pain in the ass, is all."

I opened my mouth to say that I could sympathize, but he went on. "Like today, I ran down to those rocks all day long because he wants us to be 'proactive,' because he thinks that if someone has to be rescued, the guard wasn't doing his job in the first place. Then I look like a dumb-ass, telling people they need to come in from the rocks, when they can see there's no problem."

I nodded, able to recite my dad's philosophy about life-guarding in my mind.

"So today he comes down to my tower as I'm getting back from one of my laps to the rocks, and he tells me that every time I run down there, the rest of the water isn't being watched. You just can't make the guy happy. I don't know what his problem is." Tyler shook his head. "He needs to get laid or something." I laughed, a little too loudly. "Anyway, that's the story of my life. What's yours?"

"Well—" Before I could get anything else out, I heard behind us the familiar hum of a truck on the sand. We both stopped, and I hoped desperately it was the other lifeguard. For the last few years, every summer had begun with a lecture about staying away from the guards on the beach. They were only out for one thing, etcetera, etcetera.

"Shit," Tyler said under his breath. "Speak of the devil." The truck pulled up next to me, and my dad stuck his head out. Of course.

"Hey, hon. See you met one of our rookies."

I cringed, probably visibly, both at being outed and at my dad's obvious inability to remember little details. I smiled tightly and snuck a sidelong glance at Tyler, who was fumbling for his composure. Funny, considering the way he had carried himself a few seconds earlier.

"Yeah. Dad, this is Tyler. It's actually his *second* year here, so technically he's not a rookie anymore. He was just showing me around." Tyler gave a nod. My dad looked at his red trunks, unimpressed.

"Huh. Well, if you're gonna walk around here off duty, you need to change out of your uniform first."

Tyler stammered. "Oh, y-yeah. . . . Sorry. It won't happen again." We were all silent for a few awkward seconds.

"Well, I'm headed home, hon. Why don't you hop in and I'll give you a ride back to the house?" He smiled broadly, but it wasn't a question.

"Nah. I think I'll walk." It was worth a try, seeing as we were being so civil at the moment.

He cleared his throat. "Nah. I think you should get in." Still smiling . . . "We've got a few things to take care of this evening." He looked at me straight on. Tyler shifted next to me. I was beat, unless I wanted to start a battle.

I turned back to Tyler and rolled my eyes before putting out my hand. "Well, thanks for the tour. It was nice to meet you." The faintest trace of a smirk crossed his face before he cleared his throat and shook my hand.

"You too. Stay off the rocks next time, or your dad'll kill me." We all forced a little laugh, and I walked around the truck and hopped into the passenger seat, dropping my stuff beside me. My dad pulled a U-turn around Tyler, gave him a wave, and we trundled away. I waited until we were a short distance off.

"Nice, Dad. Thanks."

"Don't start," he said flatly. "He's a lifeguard. And you're my daughter. That's as good as it gets."

"And that makes sense *how* again? I don't get it. I really don't." I paused. It was always right there, on the tip of my tongue when we had this talk. This time I said it. "You were a lifeguard when Mom married you. What was *so* bad about that?" I regretted it the instant I said it.

He didn't say anything at first. Just looked out the window. But I knew by his voice when he spoke that I'd hit a nerve. "Anna. *Don't.*"

The moment felt far more serious than I'd meant it to get. More than seemed reasonable. I looked at my lap. "Okay. I get it." I didn't at all, but I didn't want to go any further than I just had. I waved my hand casually. "It wasn't anything, anyway. I met a girl on the beach, too. She somehow talked me into joining the cross-country team. First practice is tomorrow."

He brightened a bit, but it seemed forced. "Really?"

"Yeah. She seemed nice." I watched him out of the corner of my eye as he steered us up onto the road in front of our cottage.

He put the truck in park and turned it off, then looked out at the water, sparkling gold and glassy from the setting sun. "Wanna paddle out?"

I knew that meant we were done and that we'd smooth over the surface I'd just tossed a rock into. But even the waves that crash down on the beach start out as tiny ripples, far out at sea.

They just gain strength over time.

5

My dreams made the night long. It'd been a while since I'd dreamed of her, but the effect was always the same. I'd just gotten better at dealing with it. By the time my dad poked his head into my room, I had already taken enough deep breaths to calm myself down and appear sleepy rather than shaken.

"Hey, Anna. Time to get up. Don't wanna be late the first day of practice." He was already in his uniform, coffee cup in hand.

I rubbed my eyes, wondering why in the world I had agreed to go. Dad disappeared into the hallway, and I heard his feet make their way over the wood floor to the living room. I lay back and looked at the ceiling. Meeting Ashley the day before seemed far away, and deciding to join the cross-country team out of the blue, on my first day in town, suddenly felt ridiculous. My stomach fluttered. Stupid.

I swung my legs out of bed and walked over to the pile of running clothes I had laid out the night before. Groggily I pulled on my shorts, aware that they were old and faded, just like the tank top I put on next. I sighed and tucked the red pendant that hung from my neck into it. When I bent to tie my shoes and got a good look at their cracked leather and balding soles, I resolved to get new everything before the next practice. Then I thought of Ashley and wondered if Prada made running clothes.

"See ya, hon! Have a good one!" my dad called. I heard the back door shut.

"Bye," I said to the quiet of the house. In the kitchen he'd left a bowl of steaming oatmeal and a twenty-dollar bill on the counter. I looked at the clock, shoveled a few bites into my mouth, and then grabbed the twenty and my keys and headed out the door. Our VW bus that had looked so perfect in front of the cottage now stood, slightly rusty and a little pathetic when I thought of rolling into the Coast High School parking lot. I dismissed the thought, annoyed at myself that I was already caring about what a bunch of people I had never met would think. It would be hard not to, though, if Ashley was any indication. I started the engine and crawled up the hill to the PCH, reminding myself that it didn't matter—that I had friends back home who were real, down-to-earth people. I just wished I could take them with me. Once on the highway, with the windows rolled down and the music cranked up, I started to feel a little better. Enough to even entertain the thought that joining the team could be a good thing. I didn't exactly want to spend my entire junior year alone.

The only car in the parking lot was a sparkly pearl white BMW. Had to be Ashley. Or *everyone* here was descended from privilege. I shook my head and parked my bus right next to it, kind of my own little statement—no use disguising the gulf between our backgrounds. As soon as I cut the engine, the passenger door of the BMW swung open, and Ashley waved excitedly from the driver's seat. I waved back, relieved it was her, and got out.

"Hey! I hope you don't mind, but I told you that practice started a half hour earlier than it actually does, because I wanted to make sure we got to talk first. Get in. I got you a coffee." She held up a Starbucks cup. "I read that Lance Armstrong totally drinks coffee before a workout because it gives you a big boost. If we drink it now, it should be perfect timing for our run."

As I had done the day before, I smiled and held back the laugh at the back of my throat. "Thanks." I took the coffee, ducked into the door, and sank into soft white leather. The inside of the car was warm and smelled like the perfume section of a department store.

"I got it skinny, just so you know."

"Skinny?"

"You know, nonfat milk, sugar-free vanilla?" she said nonchalantly. "Anyway, you didn't eat breakfast, right, because this will be our first calorie-burning run."

"Nope," I lied. "Nothing but fat to burn here." I patted my stomach, wondering if it pooched out at all.

"Good." She looked in the rearview mirror as another car pulled up. I was relieved that it was a nondescript black something-or-other. "Oh, that's Jillian. She's supposed to be really fast. Her sister was faster, though, but she died in a car accident a few years ago." She pulled a tube of mascara out of her purse and began applying it in the rearview mirror. "So. Sad."

"How do you *know* all this? I thought you were new." I eyed Jillian as she got out of her car. She was average-looking—brown hair in a ponytail, regular running clothes, serious expression, confident walk. Nothing out of the ordinary. It made me wonder how I looked to people who knew about my mom.

"New to the *school*. I've lived here all my life. My brother graduated from here last year. He ran for them." She finished with her mascara and moved on to a tube of lip gloss. "He talked to Coach Martin yesterday, and he's expecting us."

"What's he expecting?" I picked nervously at the edge of my plastic coffee lid. Before I finished my question, a white truck pulled up. The driver was a man, midforties, who wore a baseball cap and sunglasses. Ashley shoved her lip gloss into her bag.

"That's him. Come on!" She squeezed my leg and hopped out of the car, waving to Coach Martin like he was a long-lost friend. He didn't look up from whatever he was fumbling with on the seat of his truck. I sighed and put my coffee cup in the holder, then swung my legs out of the car.

A few more cars had pulled up, and girls—juniors and seniors, I assumed—got out and greeted each other. It was easy to see which ones hadn't seen each other in a while by the enthusiastic hugs and instant chatter. None of them wore makeup like Ashley, and that made me feel better, like I might actually be in the right place. Like *she* might be the one who was out of place. Girls milled around in twos and threes, absently stretching and shaking out their legs as they talked. No one said anything to us.

It was earlier than I wanted to be awake, but I was abuzz with nervous energy. I kicked my foot up behind me and stretched my quad. Ashley, who stood next to me in hot pink running shoes and an outfit to match, looked over and did the same. Almost. When she grabbed her foot, she wobbled for a split second before using me as her last hope to avoid hitting the asphalt of the school parking lot. We both went down with a thud, and Coach Martin finally looked at us. He walked over casually.

"Miss Whitmore. This must be your friend I heard about." He looked directly at me. "What's your name?" It felt like a trick question.

"Anna Ryan. I just moved here from up north. I, uh . . ." I fumbled, not sure if I should add more. He stared, waiting for me to finish. I had been right about the midforties guess. Silver hair peeked out from under his hat, and I was sure that if he'd taken off his glasses, his eyes would have shown his age. In any case, he had an athletic build that looked like he meant business. "I . . ."

Luckily, he rescued me. "You want to run, right?" I nodded. "Well, let's see what you can do. Miss Whitmore, I'll be watching to see what you can do too." His voice carried a note of sarcasm that set off a few knowing glances among the girls. I watched, trying to get a read on whether those glances applied to me by default, since I'd showed up with Ashley. Nice as she was, I wasn't sure I wanted to be put in the same category they'd probably decided she belonged in.

Coach Martin turned to the group of runners now gathered in front of him, and stood silent until everyone settled, all eyes on him. "Ladies, welcome to Hell Week. Double days this week, Monday through Friday. You'll take a break over the weekend, then our kickoff meet will be at the end of the first week of school. This morning we'll be running Poles." He pointed to the ridge behind him. Stifled groans rippled through the group. "You'll go out together on the first mile, but once you get to the hill, I want to see what you can do. It's your chance to make the first impression of the year. All of you." His eyes flicked to me and Ashley, and I felt his challenge knot up in my stomach. Clearly, he (and the rest of them) thought we were a joke. I willed the knot down, like I always had, breathed deeply, and resolved to prove him wrong. He gulped his coffee. "Now get stretched out. You have five minutes."

Everyone backed into a large circle, and Jillian led us through a series of stretches that I did without focus as I eyed the hill that loomed above us. I had actually always liked hill runs, because you had to run up them hard and fast or else the hill beat you. Those were short, steep hills. Poles was a monster of a hill, though. All the way up, no flats or switchbacks or anything. A pure guts run. I breathed deeply through my nose, then bent to touch the ground, stretching my hamstrings.

"All right, that's it." Jillian stood and shook out her legs. "Let's go."

I set my jaw. Ashley gave me a nudge and a confident nod. Coach Martin blew his whistle, and we were off. The pack started at a slow, casual jog, but nobody spoke. Except for Ashley, who was on my right.

"So." She took a breath as our feet pounded the dirt road. "Where did you move here from anyway?"

I kept my eyes on Jillian, who was a few runners ahead of us. "Pismo Beach. North of here."

"Oh," she breathed. The pace was picking up already. Nobody had said anything, but I could definitely feel it and it was obvious that Ashley could too. "Why?" It was all she could manage at this point.

"Dad's job." I looked sideways at her. She was already leaning forward, hard. Lurching actually. I continued, comfortable with our cadence. "Lifeguard supervisor. Runs Crystal Cove now. It's why I was down there."

"Oh. And . . . what about . . . your mom? What . . . does . . . she do?"

I coughed and picked up the pace, hoping to just leave the question behind. I didn't want to explain it here, now, to someone I barely knew.

Ashley was breathing heavily now and had started to slump her shoulders forward and tilt her chin up. I looked from her to Jillian, who looked as comfortable as I felt. We neared the base of the hill, and the incline increased with every foot strike. I felt my legs want to speed up into it.

"So?" Ashley huffed.

"So what?" I replied.

"What about . . . your mom? What's . . . she do?" When she looked over at me, I saw her carefully applied makeup beginning to melt.

"She's away a lot. Hey, you mind if I pick it up? I need some momentum for this hill."

Ashley looked relieved and immediately stopped running. "Yeah. I think I'm going to save my momentum for the top." She fanned herself. "I'll catch up." She smiled. "In a few hours."

I nodded and accelerated, then felt the bite of the hill as it rose upward steeply. The majority of the group had done the same, and we all shifted into work mode. I looked at the peak of the hill, then put my head down and let my eyes follow the dirt trail. It wasn't often that I ran somewhere other than the beach, with its familiar sound of the waves rolling into the shore. Here, on this hill, I could only hear the crunch of our shoes on dirt and my breathing, which had become hard and steady.

My legs and chest burned, and I thought about why I had lied to Ashley. It was a normal enough question. It just happened to be that the answer was one that would inevitably lead to shock, then pity, and then awkward moments as she tried to figure out where to go from that point in the conversation. It was nobody's fault. That's just how it was. It was a relief to be able to brush it off and not go there. It dawned on me as another advantage of starting over. I didn't need to have those moments if I didn't want to. I could say whatever, and nobody would be the wiser. A surge of energy pushed me forward, and I approached Jillian, who had pulled ahead of the group.

She heard my feet and looked over her shoulder. She dug in a little more, despite our hard uphill pace. I matched it. When we were shoulder to shoulder, I looked over and nodded. Her eyes flicked sideways, but she didn't acknowledge me. The small snub was enough for me to decide I had to beat her. We leaned into the hill, at a pace that would be hard to hold the rest of the way. I picked it up ever so slightly and concentrated on controlling my breathing. When she matched me instantly, I started to regret the move.

The two of us locked into a pace of hard resolve. My legs ached. My chest burned. I looked out of the corner of my eye, hoping to see a sign of the same fatigue in Jillian. She had her head down and seemed to be concentrating on the dirt directly in front of her, completely unaware of me. I forced myself to do the same, knowing it would take less energy. But then I felt her eyes on me, and all I wanted to do was look perfectly relaxed, perfectly at home on this hill that felt as if it stood up more vertical with each step. I glanced at the top and hoped that what I was about to do wouldn't bite me in the ass. She was still looking at me, trying to determine how much I was hurting.

I turned my head so that I was looking right at her, and forced my face to relax into a smile. "Hey. I heard you're the fastest on the team."

She didn't respond, except to focus her eyes straight ahead, on the peak, which was indicated by the final telephone pole.

"So . . . you must have been running a long time."

No response.

"Huh. Well. I'm feeling pretty good, so I'm gonna go for it now. I'll see ya up there." Her head shot in my direction. I took advantage and put everything into a forward surge that moved me a few paces ahead of her. I heard an out-of-breath swear and then the quickening of her feet on the dirt. I was already at a pace I could barely hold, but pride took over, and the top of the hill was just within reach, so I gave it everything I had left and focused on keeping her out of my periphery.

Then I saw her brown hair. The rest of her frame followed, and in a second she was a footfall in front of me. Jillian looked back and smiled, then full-out sprinted the last twenty-five yards. She was walking small circles when I crossed the chalked line at the top. I wanted to crumble to the ground, but I forced myself to stagger forward and walk it off.

Coach Martin walked over slowly, his steps measured out by the slow claps of his hands. "Well done, ladies. That was quite a battle."

I bent over, hands propped on my knees, and didn't say anything. My necklace swung out from under my top and dangled, shiny and red. I just watched it and tried not to heave up my oatmeal.

"Anna, is it? I guess you should formally meet the senior who just handed you your ass." He turned and put a hand out. "This . . . is Jillian." He turned to her. "And, Jill, you should formally meet the new girl who *almost* handed you yours."

We looked at each other and breathed, expressionless, and waiting to see who would look down first. Then she stood up and stuck out a hand. "Good one. You run like something's chasing you."

I grabbed it and managed a smile. "*You* were, for a few seconds." She smiled back, and we shook once before she turned her attention to the other runners, who stepped across the chalk line. She cheered for them, hands to her mouth. Some walked it out. Others bent over. One gave me a nod. Everyone looked like they hurt.

Coach Martin clapped his hands again. "All right, ladies. Good effort up here this morning. Hope you saved some for this afternoon, though. We'll be doing a long, slow distance run. Head on down, get a drink, and don't let yourselves get too tight before the afternoon. Good job."

We all started down the hill.

"Anna, you got a second?" He motioned for me to step over to him, then took his glasses off. I waited.

"What you just did back there was pretty impressive—"

"Thanks," I breathed, still tired out.

"I haven't seen Jill run like that . . . well, for a while. You got her guts up, and that was good to see. Nicely done. We'd be happy to have you. Now go rest up for this afternoon."

"Okay. Thanks, coach." I turned on shaky legs and made my way down the hill with a vague feeling that I knew what he meant about Jillian. I was still annoyed at getting beaten, but I entertained the possibility that maybe we'd even end up friends.

When I got to the bottom, Ashley's car was already idling in the parking lot. I peeked in the passenger window. She lay fully reclined in the driver's seat, almost completely covered with blue gel ice packs. She had a green eye mask over her eyes. I could hear the muffled sound of music but couldn't quite make out what it was.

I knocked. She didn't startle, didn't sit up or even uncover her eyes. She simply extended an arm and motioned languidly for me to open the door. As I did, the smell of lavender poured from the car, along with the voice of a man telling us to breath deeply into our heart centers.

"Hey—"

Her hand jolted up abruptly, in the motion of a crossing guard. It was too much. I lost it and burst into a laugh, finally. She sat up, and the green cucumber gel mask fell off her face.

"You totally interrupted my meditation."

"I'm sorry," I managed.

A slow smile spread across her red face. "I know. Don't worry. It's just that I heard somewhere that visualizing yourself doing something is the first step to doing whatever it is. I thought I could start with breathing and running at the same time. You wanna get in?"

I looked down at the white leather. "No, it's okay. I'm all sweaty. I was just coming over to tell you that we have another run this afternoon. A 'long, slow distance run.'"

She scrunched her nose. "Maybe I'll be better at that. I can do slow. I just don't know about the 'long' part."

I flexed my foot in front of me. "Yeah. It's gonna hurt after that hill. I think I'm going to get something to eat and then hang out on the beach until then. You wanna come down?"

"Oh, I wish I could, but I have a cleansing massage scheduled, and then I have to take my dog to her psychologist."

Had she not been so matter-of-fact, I would have thought she'd decided I wasn't worth hanging out with. But I figured nobody would make up something that ridiculous-sounding. "Okay. See you at four, then. Rest up."

"Sounds good." She smiled. "Try to eat as little as possible today before the next run!"

"Yeah, will do." I closed the door and headed over to my bus, already feeling my legs tightening up. The twenty in my purse wouldn't come close to getting me a massage, but it could get some lunch. I immediately thought of the smells from the Beachcomber the morning before, and decided to treat myself after a shower. On the highway, ocean air rushed in through the open windows and swirled all around me. I turned up my music, stuck my hand out the window, and flew the bus all the way home.

The rest of Hell Week flew by in a blur of running, eating, and sleeping. The eating became my big inside joke with myself. Ashley continually showed up at practice, consistently didn't finish the runs, and always kept tabs on what I had eaten that day. She was very considerate that way. I tried to help her out with the whole running thing, but it turned out that she didn't much like exerting herself. Still, she showed up to practice and began creating a role for herself there. Kind of a team cheerleader/fashion consultant/new age guru. It would take a little while, but I could see her slowly winning over the team, and even Coach Martin. Jillian and I continued the friendly rivalry we'd started on the first day, and one day, after a beach run, she even stayed after the rest of the girls had gone. We sat on the beach, people watching and tossing pebbles into the water. We talked mostly surface stuff—running and school, and I got the feeling she might actually want to be friends but was the kind of person who held people at a distance for a while first. I understood, and it felt like another thing we had in common.

Between practices I spent my days on the beach trying to soak up the last week of sun and summer before the start of school. And hoping to run into Tyler again. Each day when I came home, I checked the tower closest to our cottage. Not that I had any sort of chance at this point. I hadn't seen or talked to him since we'd met. But the possibility brought me down to the beach in a different bikini every day, sore legs and all. I walked a bit, looking for glass. I jumped into the water when it got too hot. Sometimes I tried to read. Mostly I drifted in and out of sleep with the sounds of the ocean and the kids around me making their way into my dreams.

My dad seemed happy that I had settled in. When he got home in the evenings, he would either go out for a dive or just paddle out and sit on his board, watching the sun go down. We barbecued and ate at our peeling red picnic table every night, listening to the crickets and the ocean. It was easy and seemingly peaceful, and we both left it at that.

From our back patio, though, I could just see the sagging roof of the beach cottage on the sand below. Every night we sat out there, I almost asked him to tell me about it, but something stopped me. Aside from the night we'd arrived, he avoided talking about the cottages so much that it seemed obvious. And I knew from experience that if he didn't want to talk about something, we didn't.

Still, each night when I flipped off the living room light, I stood for a minute in our warm living room, staring out the giant window at the dark silhouette of the abandoned cottage, waiting. For something.

6

On Saturday morning I lay in bed long after I was awake, because I could. The sun shone brightly through my shades and lit up the room, golden and warm. My dad had the day off, and I listened as he made his coffee and shuffled around before settling down somewhere. When I got up, he was sitting on the couch, cup of coffee in hand, watching the water.

"Mornin'." He nodded at the window. "Check that out." I looked out just in time to catch three silvery dolphin fins surface and then dip below again.

Smiling, I stretched my arms above my head. "Yeah, they've been out here every morning this week." I shook off a yawn and sat sideways in the armchair, hanging my legs over the arm so I could face the ocean. It had become a favorite spot of mine. On the sand, families were already starting to stream down, lugging ice chests and umbrellas. A pair of little girls, still in their sundresses, ran circles around each other as their parents unfurled a bright red beach blanket and then smoothed the lumps of sand beneath it. Out in the water, beyond the lifeguard buoy, an outrigger canoe glided over the morning glass, its paddlers perfectly in sync. After the week's endless workouts, I couldn't think of anything better than being out there on the beach all day, doing absolutely nothing.

"You wanna go out on Andy's boat today? We're taking it out paddy-hopping, looking for sea bass. You wouldn't have to dive. You could just stay on the boat if you wanted, or you could come with us." My dad was grinning like he always did when he got together with Andy. I weighed the idea. "C'mon. He hasn't seen you in almost a year, since he was up last Christmas."

Andy was my surrogate uncle, Dad's best friend since elementary school. Together the two of them were ridiculous and perfect, and the closest thing to a family I had, besides my grandma. Andy had never left this area like my dad did, but had always made the trek up north to see us on holidays and vacations. I loved him dearly, but it wasn't what I had in mind.

"I don't know." I rubbed my eyes. "I was kinda looking forward to just hanging out here for the day."

My dad shook his head. "You'd like it out there in the big blue. You're gonna be sitting on the beach later today, and all of a sudden have a feeling that you're missing out on something." He set his coffee cup on the table and looked at his watch. "You have an hour to change your mind. I'm gonna get my gear packed up." He messed my hair as he walked by.

I swatted at his hand, and he did it again, trying to get a smile. "I'll think about it," I conceded. We both knew I wouldn't change my mind, but I didn't have the heart to just flat-out say no. Now that we were down here, Andy would probably become a regular fixture anyway.

"Fifty-eight minutes!" my dad yelled from the kitchen.

I turned my attention back to the beach and to the guard who was just opening his tower. The lifeguard truck waited while he undid the padlocks on the windows. Once he had it open, he jumped onto the sand and pulled a set of fins and a red buoy from the back of the truck. A hand reached out from the passenger window and gave him a radio. He climbed the ladder again, and the truck slowly trundled south to open up the next tower. I couldn't see who was inside, but I buzzed with the possibility that it could be Tyler, and I was perfectly happy to stay on the beach, with my dad far out on the ocean in a boat with his friend. Heh heh heh.

I bided my time in my chair until I saw him heave his scuba bag into the back of the bus. Dressed in trunks, a T-shirt, and flip-flops, my dad looked younger than he was. Anyone who saw him with Andy probably assumed they were just a couple of single bachelors. He came up the front steps and poked his head in the door. "Last chance to change your mind."

I leaned my head back on the chair. "Nah, I'm stayin'. Ashley might come down to hang out."

"All right. Suit yourself. He's gonna be disappointed, though. You'll hear it next time you see him, for sure."

"I know."

"Okay. I don't know how long we'll be out. There's plenty to throw together for dinner. If you go anywhere, leave me a note."

I nodded. "Bye, Dad. Tell Andy I said hi, and get some fish while you're out there."

"Will do."

As soon as he pulled out, I jumped up and went to find my bathing suit for the day. Within ten minutes I was on the sand, heading over to the mystery lifeguard in the tower. He saw me coming and came outside on the deck of it without taking his eyes from the water. I stopped in front of his ladder and squinted up at him. He kneeled down, eyes still on the water.

"Hi there. Can I do something for you?" His big, cheesy smile was further complimented by his dark brown mustache and reflective aviators.

I smiled back, tilted my head, and leaned on the tower ladder. "Hopefully. I'm looking for a guard who works here . . . Tyler." I stopped, realizing I didn't know his last name, then tried to recover. "I thought he was scheduled for this tower today."

Another smile crept across the lifeguard's face, though this time it was more mischievous. He raised an eyebrow. "He *was* scheduled for this tower . . . until our new supervisor up and shifted the schedule all around for some reason." He pushed his sunglasses back into the mass of salty-dry curls and smiled at me with eyes older than I had initially guessed he had. "You must be Anna." He stuck out a hand. "I'm James. James Miller. And I've been warned about you already."

We shook, and I smiled back, startled. "*Warned?* By who?"

"Oh"—he grinned again—"a few different sources. . . . Cute little blond girl trying to pass herself off as a regular ol' tide-pooler, when she's actually the daughter of the boss man." He took in an exaggerated deep breath. "Yep. I've heard about you. Luckily, my taste is far more sophisticated . . . like Mona here." He motioned to a woman jogging through the soft sand. Her skin shone, brown and oiled, except for her face, which was shaded under a running hat. Along with her resolved expression she wore a sports bra, a water belt, and bikini bottoms. She passed by the tower and nodded at James. He gave a wave and watched as she went by. When she did, there was nothing I could do but marvel. Her bikini bottom was a black thong that revealed a high, rounded butt of all muscle. "The benefits of running the beach," he muttered, shaking his head.

"Wow. She's gotta be in her forties." James nodded appreciatively, still looking. I tried to figure out how old *he* was. He carried himself like a young guy, but the lines around his eyes told a different story. He was probably a perma-seasonal, as my dad called them. Guys that started out lifeguarding for their summer jobs at sixteen and just kept on doing it and living the life. I liked James already. He was like every one of my dad's friends that came around. All of them wanted to be young forever, and at some point they neglected to realize that they weren't. We both stood and watched Mona bump farther and farther away.

"So, little Ryan." He turned to me. "You're looking for Tyler Evans, just so you know. There's about five Tylers who work here, but he's the one you sicced your dad on the other day. Unintentionally, I'm sure. He's been banished to Tower Two for the last week." I stood silently, not knowing if I should apologize or laugh. James helped me out. "Walk on down and say hi. It's the least you could do. And, hey, tonight's the end of the season lifeguard bonfire, down at Muddy Creek." He held his arms out like a circus ringleader, then bowed to me. "If he doesn't invite you, then, I have." With that he picked up his binoculars and scanned the water to the south, then swept up to the north, where I was sure Mona and her amazingly toned butt were the main points of interest.

"Thanks," I said, and turned south, toward Tower Two.

"See you tonight, sunshine!" James called out. "Bring your tiny blond friend." I turned back and put my hands to my mouth.

"She's too young for you!"

James put a hand to his chest like he had been stabbed, and staggered backward for a second before resuming his position leaning over the railing. I turned around, smiling and plotting as I walked.

It was one of the last weekends before school, and the beach was packed. Most of the sand in front of our house was claimed already, different groups marking their territory with bright beach towels and umbrellas. The tide was high and there was swell, which made the beach even smaller. I walked in the wet sand, and when a big set rolled through, the water splashed warm over my feet. Just ahead of me were the tide pools, now crawling with people, and I smiled, remembering Tyler's exasperation at running down there. James didn't seem too concerned, although today would be the day to be. The first wave of a set thundered down onto the rocks, and people let out a collective yell, then scurried for a safer spot. I kept my eyes on Tower Two, which was a long walk down the beach.

Once I passed the tide pools, the crowd thinned out and I slowed down. Directly in front of me as I walked was the point I had run to my first day here. The point where my dad had told me my parents had met. I looked down, remembering the piece of glass I'd found that first day, but the waves had scoured the sand clean. When I rounded a smaller point, Tyler's tower came into view, but I didn't see him on the deck. I straightened up and walked more carefully, just in case he happened to be looking in my direction through his binoculars. When I was sure I was close enough for him to have to notice me, I smiled and attempted to saunter over with an ease that I hoped looked believable. He came out of his tower shaking his head. I put my chin up and feigned innocence. "What?"

"Anna Ryan," he said, still shaking his head. My stomach jumped at the sound of my name spoken by his voice. "Boss's daughter . . ."

"I couldn't tell you he was my dad right off the bat. You wouldn't have given me your little tour."

Tyler's eyebrows raised behind his sunglasses as he leaned forward with an emphatic look in each direction. "Where is he, by the way? Did you tell him you were coming on down, cuz it's just about time he got down here to bug me today. And now he has a real reason."

"Funny." I rested a hand on my hip. He looked down, and I guessed that he was looking me over from behind his sunglasses, the same as I was him. I hoped he was as impressed as I was at the moment. He had the long, lean body of the swimmers I'd seen over the years, with broad shoulders and a narrow waist. I took a few steps closer and grabbed the handle of the tower ladder, then looked right up at him. "So, James told me about the bonfire tonight." He looked interested . . . or surprised. I went on, encouraged. "Where's Muddy Creek?"

He laughed and pointed down toward the south point. "Just down there, where that ramp comes down to the beach. You ran past it last weekend."

It took a second, but then I remembered the backpacks on the sand and the surfers in the water. "You were out in the water."

"And you were showing off."

He had me there.

"Somebody had to do something impressive. I didn't see you guys out there getting any waves." I winced a little, inwardly. It wasn't one of my best lines. Tyler looked back out at the empty water, apparently disregarding my lameness.

"Yeah, that day was crappy. I should be out there *today*. Look at it." He pointed to a wave that broke off a set of rocks just offshore and peeled across the little cove. "Yep, I just get to sit down here in no-man's-land and look at it all day. Courtesy of the Ryans." He leaned forward on the railing and watched another wave roll through.

I leaned my back against the ladder and looked up over my shoulder. "Sorry about that."

He laughed. "Nah, don't be. I knew what I was getting into when I talked to you."

I turned around. "Wait a sec. You *knew* who I was? Why'd you go along with it?" I was suddenly intrigued.

"James bet me I wouldn't do it because you're Ryan's daughter. He gets a laugh out of that stuff. Why'd *you* go along while I talked crap about your dad?"

I shrugged. "He drives you crazy as a boss. Imagine having him as your dad."

Tyler held on to the tower railing and leaned back, pulling his shoulders back in a stretch. "You're his daughter. He's supposed to be that way. He's been around long enough to realize that most guys are a bunch of jerks."

I rolled my eyes. "Oh, please. Now you sound just like him." This wasn't the direction I'd envisioned this conversation taking. I needed to bring his focus back to me, so I turned slowly around so that I was facing the ladder, leaned my chest against it, and looked up at him casually. "Anyway, are you going tonight? To the bonfire?"

"Yeah, I'll be there." Tyler turned to spit out a sunflower seed shell. "*You* shouldn't be, though." He cleared his throat and laughed. "That's probably why James invited you. He's a pot-stirrer."

I suddenly felt not so cute anymore, deflated, just like that. He spit another shell into the sand, then looked down the beach. *I should just turn around and walk away,* I thought. Take a hint. But his attitude pissed me off. I looked out at the water and the outline of Catalina directly in front of us. "My dad and his buddy took their boat to Catalina for the night. I think it'll be fine," I said flatly. It was probably safe. They'd gotten off to a late start and would most likely go out for beers or something afterward.

Tyler didn't take the bait. "Oh, yeah? Well, in that case he'll probably have one of his buddies checkin' in on you. Or all of us." He smiled down at me. Condescendingly, I thought. "Maybe some other time, like when we all don't have to answer to your dad."

Heat crept across my chest and settled on my face. He really didn't like me. At all. Jerk. Humility peeled my fingers from the railing while at the same time pride made me open my mouth. "Wow. I guess a middle-aged lifeguard supervisor is a pretty scary thing." Again, it wasn't all that impressive, but I had to say something. I walked away, wishing I had thought up something better.

"Bye, Anna!!" he called. I didn't turn around, but waved my hand over my head, more out of annoyance than anything else. Then I loosened my ponytail and let my hair fall down to my back, shaking it out a little with my fingers as I walked away. I had plans to make.

7

The sun dipped into the ocean as we pulled into the Muddy Creek lot. Ashley squinted behind her giant sunglasses and scanned for the best place to park.

"Does it matter where I go? I don't want to get a ticket or get carjacked or anything."

I smiled. "Nobody's gonna carjack you. Besides, if you get a ticket, I'll just have my dad take care of it."

"All right, all right. It just looks so . . . remote. Is that the right word for when it seems, like, far away or something?"

I laughed. "Yeah, that's what it means, but I wouldn't call it remote with that shopping center over there." I pointed to the lights across PCH.

"Whatever." She pulled into a spot, or rather, two spots. "I hope we brought enough goodies. I grabbed everything I could think of that would be good for a bonfire. Do you think some-one will have a corkscrew?"

"For what?"

"For the champagne. It was the best thing I could sneak out of the house. My mom has a big stash of it for her parties."

"Um, Ash, you don't need a corkscrew for champagne. You know how it pops and all?" I couldn't help but smile. "And . . . why'd you bring champagne for a bonfire, anyway?"

She looked at me like I had just asked her why the sky was blue, then said simply: "It's festive!" She pulled her lip gloss out of her purse, reapplied, and then smacked her lips. "I fig-ured there'd be some cute lifeguards to lug it down. Come on, Anna. That's supposed to be your thing."

"Yeah, we'll see," I said, looking around. "None seem to be falling at my feet just yet."

I opened the door and scanned the parking lot, hoping to see one in particular. Ashley popped the trunk of her car and walked around to the back. I couldn't help but stare for a second at the perfect magazine picture that she was. She looked like an ad for Southern California rich, with her three-hundred-dollar jeans and gauzy white top. The front sections of her blond hair were twisted back into a hippyish do that left the rest of it wavy and expertly tousled. She smiled her sunset-lip-gloss smile, and for half a second I thought about the lack of logic in bringing a beautiful, friendly girl along when I was trying to hook Tyler.

I pulled down the sun visor and checked myself in the mir-ror. I had the kind of skin that tanned easily, and by this point in the summer it was deep brown with a few freckles scat-tered across my nose and cheeks. I had always liked it when it got like this, because it meant I'd had a good summer. Ashley walked over and bent to look at my reflection with me.

"You know, MAC makes a really good makeup that would totally take care of those freckles and even out your skin tone." I looked at her immaculately made-up face.

"I didn't have time to put on any makeup. Lemme see your lip gloss." I had actually thought about it before I'd left, but then had figured it'd be dark anyway. And I didn't want to look like I was trying too hard. But then, a little bit couldn't hurt. She handed it over and I smoothed the thick cakey-smelling gloss over my lips. "Okay. Let's get the stuff and go down there."

Just as I stepped out and closed the door, a jeep pulled up next to us. It was James. "Ladies!" He leaned out of the car. "Glad you could make it. Can I help you carry anything down?"

"Sure!" Ashley interjected, before I had even opened my mouth. I gave her a look. She pranced back to her trunk excitedly and began pulling out grocery bags. "I have all kinds of stuff in here—chips and cookies, hot dogs, all the bonfire stuff I could think of. And s'mores stuff too! No dieting tonight."

James followed her to the back of the car and stood there smiling as she loaded his arms up. "You don't mess around, do you?"

She pulled out a stack of Mexican blankets and put them into my arms. "Aren't these cute? I picked them up today at Pottery Barn. Oh! And these." She handed me a bundle of tiki torches. "They're perfect, right?"

I nodded. "Ash, you didn't have to go out and get all this—"

She waved me off, then shrugged cutely. "Why not? It was fun. It will be fun. Right, James?"

"That's right!" He grinned from behind his aviators and gave an enthusiastic thumbs-up. "*Super* fun. Is that about it? We got a long walk ahead of us, and I could use an icy cold one ASAP."

Ashley shut the trunk. "That's it. Show me to the beach!" She put an arm out, and James took it, despite all he was carrying.

It was nearly impossible to be around her and not start thinking everything was just a grand adventure. As we tromped down the steep trail to the beach, I grinned and listened to Ashley chattering to James about what an admirable and heroic profession he was in, which I was sure he was eating up. They all did.

At the bottom of the trail the beach was open and empty except for a small gathering around the rock-bordered fire pit. A small pyramid of kindling sat in the middle, waiting for a splash of lighter fluid and a match. The group was mostly made up of tanned guys who stood holding red cups, barefoot in their best surf shirts and jeans. I dug my toes into the cool sand as I walked over, trying to find Tyler's face among them. James set everything down and walked around the circle of guys, giving high fives. Ashley and I stood on the outside of the ring, while a girl sitting on the sand looked both of us over as she chewed her gum. She leaned over and whispered something to her friend next to her, and they both laughed. Just as I started to rethink the idea of us being there, James raised his voice.

"Everybody, this is Anna Ryan. That would be *Boss* Ryan's daughter, so you never saw her here." He waited for a reaction, which mostly consisted of nods meant to say hi. I nodded back and wished I had a red cup in my hand to raise and hide behind. "And this is her friend Ashley, who has been so kind as to bring a giant spread of stuff for our little soiree here."

Ashley gave a coy little smile. "Anyone want to toast to any-thing? I brought a case of champagne." It was like someone had pressed play again after pausing a scene. Everyone hopped to life, and soon plastic champagne flutes were tapping, the fire was lit, and we all were feeling plenty warm, even though the night had cooled down. After a long, rambling toast delivered by James, the veteran of the group, we all settled around the fire that was now spitting and crackling.

Muted conversations drifted across the fire, then tapered off. In between, the periodic smack of a wave on the sand punctuated the easy, satisfied silences, and it felt like one of those nights so perfect, you always remember it. The breeze shifted in my direction, along with the smoke, so I stood up to avoid the burn in my eyes. With no moon illuminating the beach, everything beyond our little ring of bonfire was black. On the highway above an occasional set of headlights cruised by and illuminated the white lines of breaking waves. It had a different feel to it from the beach in Pismo, with its pier lights and busy promenade. There was a quietness here that felt unique and special.

I thought about the cottages lining the beach near my house, and of the one that sat alone on the sand. How they just sat in dark silence as the waves rushed up each night, probably all with stories to tell of perfect summer evenings. For a moment, when we'd first arrived, my dad had started to tell me about them. But I had been too mad at him about moving to listen, and since then they'd felt almost like a taboo topic. Like a lot of things were with him. Now I was curious about how it had all started, this little place that felt so separate from the rest of the world. I sat back down and asked no one in particular, "So what's the deal with all of those empty cottages near the restaurant? The ones on my side of the beach are all fixed up, but those look like people just up and left twenty years ago or something."

Next to me James cleared his throat and sighed. "Ah, the history of the cove. Let me give you the short version. A long time ago—like, back in the thirties or something—the cove was owned by a guy who leased it out to families that started out as campers. From Memorial Day to Labor Day—the whole summer." He took a swig of beer from his red cup and stifled a burp. "Eventually those people decided it was the best little piece of paradise around, and they got themselves long-term leases with him and started turning their camping spots into beach shacks. It was like a private little village with parties round the clock, and people just doing their thing—diving for dinner in the ocean, sharing everything with each other, being artsy . . . whatever. The rest of the world left them alone, and they liked it that way." He paused. "How do you not know all this, Ryan? Your dad's like a piece of living Crystal Cove history." Before I could answer, he took in a deep breath and went on.

"Anyway, fast-forward to the seventies, when the state bought the land from this landowner guy. The families got eviction notices from the state and fought them for twenty or so years until they finally lost. When they did, it got *real* ugly down here."

Ashley had stopped listening and was complimenting the gum-chewing girl on her marshmallow-roasting abil-ity. Everyone else had settled into two- or three-person con-versations around the fire. James stopped for a second and stretched. "Am I losin' you, Ryan?"

"No, no," I encouraged. "What do you mean 'ugly'?"

"I mean, they basically got kicked out of houses that had been in their families for generations. They were bitter, for sure. Some of 'em refused to leave, even on the last night, and it got so out of hand that even the lifeguards had to help out the cops to get them out. Your dad's probably got some crazy stories from that night." He looked at me for confirmation. I hadn't heard any. Couldn't even think of *over*hearing any. I'd had no idea about any of it.

I took a long drink of champagne and forced it down with a shiver. "So, then what?" Bubbles fizzed at the back of my throat.

"By the time the state got the cottages, they were historical landmarks, so they started to fix 'em up. They did all the ones on your side of the beach and up the bluff, and now they get rented out by vacationers from all over. Germans with a love for Speedos especially seem to like 'em. You notice that?"

"And the ones on the north side of the beach? And that one near my house? They look like they're about to fall down."

"They probably are. But the money ran out. They'll be fixed up one day, but not anytime soon." A few beats passed between us, and I pictured the beach cottage next to mine, with its turquoise fence and hazy windows. Stuck in time, waiting.

"Had your fill of history now? My cup's about dry. You want a refill?"

"Huh? Oh, yeah, sorry. I mean, thanks." James stood and brushed the sand off his legs. "Have you ever been in any of them?"

"Your dad has the keys to all of them," a familiar voice said from across the fire.

My stomach flip-flopped, and I ceased to care about anything else James could tell me. He immediately understood and excused himself to the keg, taking my cup with him. Tyler walked over casually and sat down next to me in the sand. I looked over and raised my eyebrows.

"Yeah?" I said. "I bet if I somehow got those keys, I wouldn't be able to find anyone brave enough to use them with me."

He took a drink from his cup. I leaned into him, just slightly, and smiled. The champagne had made me bold. "In fact, isn't it dangerous for you to be here, sitting next to me?" I lowered my voice to a near-whisper. "I mean, my dad's your *boss* . . ."

A slow smile crossed his face, and he put his chin down. "There are some things in life you can't miss, and this bonfire is one of them."

I looked at him, puzzled. It didn't seem like that big a deal.

"You'll see. We're only just getting started."

James returned with a red cup full of champagne for me, and Ashley fell giggling on the other side of me. "This is the best night! Except, do you know what? Nobody knows how to say the name of this. She held up an empty champagne bottle, its yellow label obscured by sand. I wiped it away with my thumb, and she pointed. "See, it's French. You say it 'vuv-clee-ko.' And you sound very sophisticated that way." We both laughed, tapped our cups, and drank. I knew champagne wasn't exactly supposed to be chugged, but I could tolerate the taste of it better than beer, and it did seem "festive," as Ashley had put it earlier, so I finished off the refill James had gotten me in a few gulps, and told myself that was it for the night.

Tyler had gotten up and was making his way around the bonfire, shaking hands and nodding with some guys, slapping others on the back. Fire crackled, and I leaned back on my hands, face to the sky, where I was surprised at how many stars I could see. It felt good to move out of reach of the heat. My cheeks still burned a bit, but I figured it was from the last few swigs of champagne. I tipped my head back to level and spun a little. Ashley put her head on my shoulder.

"Anna?"

"Yeah?"

"I think I'm drunk."

"Me too." She hiccupped, and we both laughed. I watched Tyler across the fire, talking with a blond kid who had to be a rookie. Tyler stood with one hand in his pocket, the other holding his red cup. Everything about him looked easy and relaxed. Confident. Like he knew I was on the other side of the fire watching his every move, and he didn't care in the least. He glanced over, right at me for a split second, and I looked away, gathering my courage.

8

James stood up and cleared his throat, over and over, until everyone realized they were supposed to look at him. I looked over at Tyler, who was grinning at this. James was wearing a straw cowboy hat and no shirt now. In the light of the fire he could pass for a twenty-year-old, but I figured he had to be at least thirty. He swept his arms out again, in a gesture meant to get everyone's attention.

"Ladies and Gentlemen, I apologize for interrupting all of the pre-hook-up groundwork that's being laid right now, but we've come to a very important point in the evening, an honored Crystal Cove lifeguard tradition."

Four of the youngest-looking guards groaned and looked at each other.

James nodded. "Yep, it's the CCAD. For you rooks, that's the Crystal Cove Ab—as in 'Ab Rock'—Dive." He pointed to the cliff at the end of the cove, the one I had run to on my first morning.

"Aw, shit," the youngest rookie muttered to the guy sitting next to him. The other guards, Tyler included, clapped their hands and hooted.

"Yep, guys. It's swim, dive, and be naked, for tomorrow you are rookies no more." None of them moved. They just sat there, waiting for further instruction. "But first," James said, looking at me for a moment, "I'm going to fill you in on a little history you may not know about, tell you all how this tradition started." He took a step closer to the fire, and everyone leaned in, smiling and trying to figure out what was gonna come out of his mouth next. He had that effect on people. James put his hands together. "Okay. It all started a long time ago—twenty years or something, I don't know. There was only one rookie that year, and he was a crazy-ass kid. I mean, this kid kicked everyone's butt swimming, towed a boat out of the surf line his second day in a tower, and pulled *crazy* tail." Everyone laughed.

"Sounds like you, James!" a voice from the other side of the fire yelled.

"Nope. I wish I was as cool as this guy was. And *Jesus*, I'm not *that* old."

"How old are you, anyway?" the same voice yelled.

"Old enough to know when to shut up. I'm trying to tell a story here." He smiled and squatted down so the fire lit up his face under the hat. "Anyway, the older guards decided this kid needed his ego knocked down a tad, so at the bonfire out here, they gave him all the beers he wanted, then threw down a challenge for him. See Ab Rock down there?" He pointed toward the rock at the end of the cove. "They told him that every year, in order to graduate from being a rookie, you had to

swim out to it, climb up to the first point, and jump off naked."
The rookies were quiet now, trying to shrink into the sand, and
I was glad I wasn't one of them. James went on.

"So anyway, the kid agreed, dropped his shorts right there in
front of the whole bonfire, and dolphin-dove out into the water.
A few of the older guards swam out with him, to make sure he
didn't chicken out. They all climbed the rock, but when they
got to the jumping point, the crazy bastard kept climbing, all
the way up to the top of the cliff, which is about fifty feet up.
At high tide." He paused and turned—and so did all of us—to
the cliff that loomed above the water. In the dark I could just
make out the outline of it, but my memory of it from that first
morning was that it would have been a scary jump to make. A
quiet resignation had settled over the rookies seated at James's
feet, and the other guards, Tyler included, stood over them,
smiling.

"Well, the goddamn kid got all the way to the top, stood
there a minute in the moonlight, naked and proud, and then
backed up, took a running head start, and launched himself
off the top of good ol' Ab Rock." He let the image sink in for a
second before he continued. "Now, everybody was waiting for
him to come up, but he decided to have some fun of his own
and come in hugging the edge of the cliff in the shadow, where
they couldn't see him. They all got worried and started diving
around for the kid. Guards on the beach jumped in. Girls were
crying. And you know what he did? He came out of the water,
still buck naked, grabbed one of the cottage girls, and laid a
big ol' wet kiss on her." James looked over at me. "And legend
has it that it was love at first kiss, because that girl became his
wife later on.

"So, how 'bout it, boys? Tonight's the night you become

men and carry on the tradition started so many years ago by our very own Boss Ryan. So strip down. Nudity is required for rookies. Evans, you collect their boxers at the waterline. The rest of you have earned the right to your shorts, if you wish. I will be jumping naked, in support of these poor saps." The veteran guards again cheered and raised their cups, and the rookies stood up, resigned to their fate.

I didn't move. People elbowed each other around me, laughing. Ashley was saying something, James and Tyler were walking over to us, and I didn't move. I sat spinning, marveling. I'd known they'd met at the cove, but that was it. Not that my dad had been this reckless and wild kid, not that my mom had been a—"cottage girl." Had she stayed here? *Lived* here? Ashley's hand on my shoulder interrupted all of the questions that swirled around. She was still giggling.

"So that crazy kid was your dad? And the girl he grabbed was your mom? That's the *cutest* story! They must love to tell it!"

I nodded, staring down into the fire. "Yeah, it's an old family favorite."

James bent down to me and Ashley. "You ladies, of course, are exempt from this requirement of the party. Although you're more than welcome to join in."

Ashley pulled a blanket over her shoulders. "I think I'll wait right here." She looked over at the rookies, who were now down to their underwear. "Are any of them cute enough for a kiss? Maybe one is my future husband."

"Not likely," replied James. "If you'll excuse me, I need to go disrobe." He tipped his straw hat, winked, and walked off down to the waterline, where everyone had gathered. I looked from the inky blackness of the water to the towering silhouette of Ab Rock, and then stood.

"Wait up! I'm in." I got up and in one swift motion pulled my sundress over my head. I wasn't going to get naked, but I figured my bra and underwear were pretty much the same thing as a bathing suit. I needed to clear my head.

Ashley turned and looked up at me, giggles gone. "Anna! You're gonna, like, die out there or something, and then it'll be this big tragedy, and then I'll miss you—"

"Come on, Ryan. We're waiting!" James yelled.

"Relax, Ash. I can handle myself." My voice came out flat, and I flashed on James's story. "I'm like a mermaid."

Everyone stood on the beach facing the water, and I was glad, because the only thing James was wearing was his straw cowboy hat and a whistle around his neck. He lifted the whistle to his lips and blew. The four rookies I had seen at the fire, plus two more who had probably been hiding, dropped their boxers, and everyone ran out into the water.

It was a sloppy mess at first, naked white butts and all. I was surprised at how uncoordinated I felt when I first dove in, and I hoped that being in the water would clear the champagne haze in my head. I dove under and opened my eyes to nothing but fuzzy black. I forced myself to concentrate on the coolness, which was enough to sober me up a bit but not to keep me from thinking of here. Here. A cottage girl. When I came up through the glassy surface, I was in the middle of the group of shiny heads. I treaded water for a second, trying to pick out Tyler.

"Hey." He swam up from the side. "You okay out here?" He was close enough for me to see the water droplets on his face.

"Yeah. I'm fine. I'm my father's daughter, remember." I said it with such bite, Tyler seemed puzzled. I couldn't even begin to describe how I felt about my dad at the moment. Instead I pulled myself forward in the water, and Tyler went with me.

I turned to him and tried to brighten my tone. "So, you had to do this last year?"

"Yep." He nodded, went under, and then resurfaced a few feet in front of me. "It's a long way down from up there. Longer if you get the landing wrong. You gonna jump?"

I turned over onto my back and kicked. "Tradition is tradition, right?"

"All right, then. Let's go."

At this we both settled into an easy freestyle stroke and pulled ahead of the group. As we neared the rock, it grew taller, the face of it steeper. I concentrated on swimming and willed myself to have the guts to follow through on the jump. When we got to the base, Tyler and I treaded water and looked straight up. I had to tilt my head way back to see the top of the rock. The surge of a wave pushed us gently into it, and I kicked back off with the balls of my feet.

Tyler turned to me. "Okay. The next surge that comes through, ride it and use it to get up onto that little ledge." He pointed to the faint outline a few feet above us. "That's the best place to start." I nodded, and just as I did, I felt the water pull away from the rock. "Okay," he said. "Get ready. . . . Now." The water surged back up to the face of the rock, and I went with it, surprised at how high it brought me. I reached for the ledge and grazed it with my fingers, but slipped back down with the water. Tyler grabbed on and pulled himself up, just as the rest of the guys caught up.

I wasn't gonna miss it a second time, in front of everybody. When the next wave rose under me, I gave one strong kick and propelled myself up to the ledge, then clamped down hard with my fingertips.

James hooted. "Yeah! Looks like it runs in the family! Go, girl." My arms shook as I pulled myself up, and I was happy that I didn't need the hand Tyler had extended down to help me. I popped up next to him on the ledge and brushed my hands off on the backs of my legs.

He nodded. "Not bad." I felt his eyes on me for a long moment, and I held them until he looked away, to the top of the rock. "It's not too bad to get up there. It's more of a slant than straight up and down, and there's plenty of spots to grab on the way up. Just don't look back once you've started. And let me know if you need any help. The first point is just up here. You can jump that one if you don't want to go all the way up."

"No. I'm going from the top. And I'm gonna jump first." I surprised myself with this, but I figured whatever I said I'd have to back up once I got up there.

"All right, then. Let's go."

I followed his lead and pulled myself up the side of the rock. Beneath us, the other guards were timing the swell to get up to the first ledge. Hoots and hollers broke through the murmurs below as they made their way up the rock behind us, completely naked. I could only be happy that I was in front of them, not having to look up. Instead I got to look up at Tyler, who I had a feeling was slowing down so that I could keep up. As with everything else, he climbed effortlessly. I concentrated on trying to look as at ease as he did, but the higher we got, the harder it was to do. It was a lot farther up than I had imagined, but there was no backing out at this point. Now I was sober.

"Almost there," Tyler said over his shoulder. "You still sure you wanna do this? Hope so, cuz climbing *down* this thing would be a bitch."

"I said I'm in." I pulled myself up and found a foothold. I took a deep breath and tried to think calm thoughts. The water had looked deep in the daylight. Plenty deep. We wouldn't be doing this unless they knew it was deep enough. I looked up, and Tyler was standing above me, his arm extended down again. This time I grabbed it, and he pulled as I pushed with my legs. In a second I was on my knees at the top of Ab Rock. I stood, carefully.

The smell of the ocean was stronger up here, the air cooler. Tyler sat down easily on the rock, his legs dangling over the edge. I shivered a little and sat next to him, close. We both looked up at the same time. There was scarcely more sky than stars. The Milky Way spread out, a faint white path above us. Tyler didn't say anything, and I kept my face upturned to the sky, waiting, hoping for him to lean into me or brush his hand against my leg. Something.

Muffled voices drifted up from below, getting closer as the rest of the guys made their way up the rock. He turned to me, then looked down, smiling. "Um . . . they'll be up here in a second. So if you wanna be the first to jump, now's the time."

I sucked in a breath and tried not to sound like the perfect moment had just been lost. "Yeah. Guess it's time." A faint wisp of potential still lingered, and we sat a few seconds longer until it dissipated into the night.

When I stood, nervous energy replaced my disappointment. I looked down into a mirror galaxy of stars on the water's surface. They danced on the ripples, and it was silent but for the gentle lapping of the water on the rocks. A cool, swirling current of air came up from below. I turned to Tyler. "You're sure it's safe? Nothing I need to avoid down there or anything?"

"It's fine. Nothing but a bottomless pool. I've dived it a million times. Just back up, take a few steps, and go straight off the edge. Trust me."

I did.

I looked down again and took a deep breath. The voices of the rest of the group were right below us. Tyler nodded and motioned toward the water with his head. I bit my lip as I backed up a few paces, then stopped and let resolve settle over me. I started with one big step, then momentum propelled me forward. Straight forward, I hoped. As my back foot left the rock, hoots and hollers echoed from below.

Time slowed down instantly, and I felt the surprising ease of plummeting. The stars shone below me, wavy on the water, and I had time to think that nothing could be more beautiful. When I sliced through the surface, warm water enveloped me. I opened my mouth and let out a squeal. Bubbles poured out and sailed upward, and then . . . quiet. I closed my eyes and drifted toward the surface, wanting to keep the quiet peace I felt right at that moment. Just before I surfaced, I heard the unmistakable sound of Tyler plunging in a few feet away from me.

I came up and looked at Ab Rock. Far above me, I could just make out James's cowboy hat. He waved his arm. "Ryan, that was awesome! Way to show these guys how it's done. Now move so they can try to top you!"

Tyler popped up next to me, grinning. "Hey," he said, a little out of breath. "What'd you think?"

I looked up again at the top of the cliff against the backdrop of stars. "That was the best thing I've ever done," I breathed.

James yelled from the top. "You guys clear? We gotta get this going. We're shriveled up here."

Tyler and I side-stroked out of the way and treaded water, keeping our eyes up. With a "Yee-haw!" James came sailing over the edge of the cliff, tucked into a cannonball. Just before he hit the water, he straightened out and held both hands over his crotch. He cut through the surface, leaving a small splash and swirls of water behind him. His hat sailed down and landed with a tiny splash, then bobbed on the ripples.

After him came a stream of naked guards, all streaks of brown and white. Everyone came up euphoric and energized. I floated on my back, still marveling at the stars, while Tyler treaded water next to James and they congratulated each guy on being a rookie no longer. When everyone had finished and it came time to head in, Tyler swam over to me.

"I'm impressed. You're the first girl I've seen take that jump, and you took it like a man."

"Thanks, I think." I dipped my chin into the water and blew bubbles. "Thanks for climbing up there with me."

"Yeah, sure." He motioned toward the shore, where we could see the silhouettes of the few people who hadn't gone out. A spotlight flashed on and panned across the water in our direction. It was mounted to a lifeguard truck. The air went out of me.

"Shit," I whispered, all euphoria zapped instantly.

"I thought he was at Catalina." Tyler's voice echoed the feeling in my stomach.

"So did I," I lied. "Shit." My mind raced. "Okay. Don't swim in with me. Stay back with those guys. Actually, you guys should go back over to the edge of the rock and come in that way. Let me deal with him." We had stopped swimming forward and were facing each other. Tyler was shaking his head, trying to hide a smile.

"I thought I said something about you coming to this party being a dumb idea . . ."

"Yeah, I know. Thanks."

"Maybe he'll be proud of you for carrying on the tradition he started." He was nearly laughing now.

"Yeah, I'm sure he'll be stoked when I get out of the water in my bra and panties smelling like champagne." I was in for it. "Save yourself," I said flatly.

He didn't move. I didn't either. I could feel another moment creeping up on us, and I willed him to just tilt his head in and kiss me before I had to swim in and deal with what waited for me on the beach. But he didn't. And too quickly I found myself kicking away through the black water, regretting that I didn't either.

9

I took my time on the way in because I knew it wouldn't be pretty once I got there. Not because of what he was going to say to me. Because of everything that he hadn't. When I stepped a firm foot on the sand and walked out of the water, it was with purpose.

My dad stood, arms crossed, leaning against his truck. The fire ring was empty. The only indications that there had actually been people there were the red cups strewn around the outskirts of it, and a few empty champagne bottles lying on their sides in the sand. The clothes piles of the swimmers were too far off from the fire ring to be visible, and I was thankful for that.

I walked straight to the truck, arms crossed over my bra, and looked my dad in the eye as best I could. He threw a towel at me and said in a low, controlled voice, "Get in."

I stood still, arms crossed. "Where's Ashley?"

His tone stayed even. "She got a ride. Get. In." I didn't move, but my mind raced, trying to find a place to start. "Now." He opened his door and sat down. My face burned. I didn't say anything but grabbed my dress and stomped over to the passenger side of his truck. I threw my stuff onto the seat between us, sat down roughly, and slammed the door. He shoved the truck into gear, and we crawled up the beach without saying anything.

After a long moment he turned to me and spoke again in the same low, controlled voice. "You smell like alcohol. You're in your underwear. And you were at a party with the exact people I specifically said you weren't to be around." He looked back out the windshield.

I knew I was asking for a fight, but it would be easier if he wasn't so calm. "Yeah, Dad. And you know what I found out tonight? That a long time ago you did the exact same thing. Oh, wait. You were actually *naked* and *drunk*, according to the story. So don't get all pissed off. I'm not drunk, and I didn't die or have sex or do anything but jump off the same rock you did—"

"Christ, Anna! You jumped off Ab Rock!" He was yelling now, and the force of it startled me. "Do you know how idiotic—" He slammed his hands on the steering wheel. "Goddamnit—"

I cut him off. "You about done?" He went deadly silent, and my courage almost left me. I lowered my own voice. "Because I heard the rest of the story too. And there's a lot you left out. Like *how* you met Mom."

In the faint light from the dashboard, I could see his jaw clench, and it was enough for me to go on.

"James called her a 'cottage girl,' Dad." He was silent, and

I almost hated him for it at that moment. "What does that *mean*? Did she *live* here? In one of those cottages? Did you think I *might* want to know something like that?" My voice had gone shrill and high, and I felt tears welling up, hot and angry.

He kept one hand on the wheel and brought the other up and rubbed his forehead. I saw him suck in a breath before he spoke. "Yeah," he said. "She stayed here. In one of the cottages."

I stared straight ahead, watching the now blurred headlights dip up and down over the sand. When I spoke again, it came out icy.

"Which one?"

He slowed, almost to a stop on the sand in front of our place, and when the motion light of the beach cottage clicked on, his voice was weary. "That one." He didn't need to point.

I lost it.

"Jesus, Dad! Why would you not tell me something like that? You didn't think I'd want to know that we're living next to Mom's old house? What else don't I know about my own *goddamn* mother?" I yanked on the door handle and shoved my shoulder into it, but it didn't budge. My hands fumbled around for the button, and when I couldn't find it, I leveled my eyes straight at him, breathing hard. "Unlock it."

"Anna—"

"Unlock it. I can't talk to you right now. I can't. Unless you want to explain what this is. Why we came here, why James knows more about my own family history than I do . . . why we don't talk about her anymore. I don't get it, Dad."

He was silent, and I stared through the blur of my tears and reflection at the now dark beach cottage that had been my mother's.

"That's what I thought," I said. "Let's don't talk about it, just like always." My hand found the unlock button, and I burst out the door, just as he finally responded. It wasn't until after I had slammed the door shut that I really heard what he'd said:

"You stopped asking."

10

It was a day for kites. The lifeguards watched over empty wind-whipped water from inside their towers as sand filled in the small valleys and smoothed itself over. I hoped none of them had been at the party the night before. I pulled my hood over my head and tied the strings so it would stay on, then headed up the beach to where I could see rocks strewn all over the sand in piles in front of the abandoned cottages. I hadn't been up this way yet, but I wasn't in the mood for sightseeing, so I kept my head down. The less I moved my neck around, the less the champagne ache wrapped itself around my head. It came in waves, alternating with nausea that made me squint behind my sunglasses. I walked the waterline like this, hands shoved into my pockets, not really paying attention to anything. I just wanted to be out of the house, where my dad and I moved around each other, silent and not knowing where to start.

A few paces ahead a freshly uncovered rock pile spread out in front of a falling-down cottage. Grateful for a distraction, I picked my way over to it but then stepped on a pebble that jabbed painfully into the arch of my foot. My foot jerked up reflexively, and as it did, I saw my first piece of glass for the day. It was a thumbnail-size green shard, still wet from the receding tide. When I lifted it and held it up to the light, it showed a deeper almost turquoise green. I rubbed its smooth edges between my thumb and forefinger inside the warmth of my sleeve and turned my attention to the surrounding sand.

"I didn't think I'd have any competition out here on a day like this," said an unfamiliar voice. I turned around. An older woman wearing only shorts and a T-shirt stood behind me, smiling. The wind whipped her waist-length brown hair around her, and she made no effort to control it.

"Oh, um, are you looking for sea glass too?"

"Yup." She motioned to the rocks. "We haven't had rock piles like this in quite a while. Yesterday's waves uncovered them."

I nodded and pulled my green piece out of my pocket. "Yeah, I just found a pretty little green one."

"May I?" she asked. I handed it to her, and she held it up to the sun between rough fingers. "Yep, that's a beauty." I smiled, and she handed it back, then reached into her pocket. Her hand rummaged around, making sure she got all of what was in it. When she brought it out and uncurled her fingers, I leaned in closer. Scattered over the palm of her hand were some of the most vibrant colors of sea glass I had ever seen. Turquoise, cobalt blue, and purple all mingled like jewels.

"Did you find all those right here, *today*?" I looked around my feet, hoping for some of her luck.

"Yeah. I told ya. It's like somebody cracked open a treasure chest." She chuckled a little. "I suppose I can share my rock piles with you for today. You seem to be someone who has an appreciation for what the ocean can uncover." She stuck out her hand. "Name's Joy. I used to live here, but now I just visit it when I can."

I wondered if when she said "here" she meant she'd been one of the residents. Who'd been forced to leave. By the state, which my dad worked for. A little wave of nervous guilt went through me, but when I took her hand, it was warm in spite of the chilling wind, and I relaxed. She had no idea who my dad was or where I lived.

I shook it. "I'm Anna." She held on, just a moment too long, her eyes studying mine, until I unclasped my hand from hers. I tucked my arms over my chest. "Aren't you cold?"

"Honey, look at me. I'm old. I haven't been cold for two years, if you know what I mean." I laughed a little, sure there must be some small joke in her comment, and thankful the strange moment had passed. "I'm gonna head up that way"—she motioned with her head—"so we don't cross paths and have to fight over the same pieces." She stepped effortlessly in her bare feet over the stones and continued on with her back to me, head down in quiet contemplation, like the rest of the world didn't exist. I stood watching, and an image of my mother walking the beach the same way opened up in my mind. I was little, maybe four or five, but the memory was vivid and one I held close and dear.

We walked together in the warm afternoon light, and every so often she would stoop to pick something up. She'd smile as she rubbed the sand off a piece of sea glass, hold it up for me to see in the sunlight, and drop it into our special blue pouch that she kept for these walks. Our walks had gotten more rare by then, but I'd wait for the days when she'd light up and ask me to join her, and we'd walk for hours.

The first piece I ever found by myself was on a walk like that. She walked ahead while I trailed a stick in the sand, watching the wavy path it made. A translucent triangle lying in the waterline caught my eye, and I bent down to investigate. White water rushed up almost to it, and I snatched it up quickly and then held it up, yelling to my mother that I had found "a beauty," just like she always called them. She turned and broke into a proud smile, then picked me up and squeezed me tight.

"This one is yours, Anna. We'll start you your own jar." I dropped it into the special pouch and carried it the rest of the way, searching for another piece, hooked on the treasure and the happiness it had brought to my mother's face. Out of all the pieces of sea glass in the jar in my room, I could still pick this one out effortlessly. It sat in the bottom of the jar, buried beneath the pieces collected over years of walking the beach without her.

Water rushed up around my feet, and beneath it I caught a flash of a slick surface. I didn't reach with my hand but put my foot down hard over the spot and waited until the water receded, leaving an indentation in the sand. I lifted my foot and bent down to retrieve the piece of glass. I didn't much care for the brown ones, but always picked them up in case they were actually red. In the sunlight I could see that it wasn't. I was about to throw it back when I saw Joy out of the corner of my eye.

"You ever heard of mermaid tears?" she asked, eyeing the piece of glass poised in my hand. When she said it, I saw my mom again, this time seated next to me while we buried our toes in the sand. She told the story while I imagined beautiful, lonely women swimming beneath the waves.

"Sea glass, right? Something to do with mermaids and sea glass."

She nodded reverently and took the piece of glass from my hand, then held it up in the wind and the sun. "The story is that each piece of sea glass that washes up on the beach is a crystallized tear that a mermaid has shed for a lost love." I could hear my mom's lyrical voice telling the same story as I sat next to her, my arms around my knees. I hadn't thought of it in forever, but the memory took shape as I listened to Joy.

She went on, turning the brown glass between her fingers. "They come from the ones who are unfortunate enough to fall in love with humans, and the mermaids are in for a lifetime of sadness because they can never be with their true loves. Only on the nights when a full moon shines on the water can they come to shore." She looked from the glass to me. "And those nights are magical, but as soon as dawn comes, they have to swim back into the ocean, leaving a trail of rainbow-colored tears behind them."

I bit my lip, silent, as images of these beautifully lonely creatures entangled themselves with flashes of my mother.

"You should never feel sorry for mermaids, though," she went on. "They've been known to take that beauty and that sadness and pull down the object of their love in a second, if given the chance. There's a poem by Yeats:

A *mermaid found a swimming lad,*
Picked him for her own,
Pressed her body to his body,
Laughed; and plunging down
Forgot in cruel happiness
That even lovers drown."

She looked out over the water, and I followed her lead. I could remember being little and thinking that mermaids were gorgeous and strong and free, because my mother had told me so. I'd gone to bed many nights wishing I would grow a tail as I slept so I could go find her, out among the waves, waiting for me.

Joy handed me back the piece of brown glass and curled my fingers around it, then looked directly at me. "I always loved the story of the mermaid tears best, though. It's stories like that that make the little things beautiful."

I blinked and swallowed a lump. "I knew that one. My mom actually told it to me a long time ago, and I kind of forgot until just now." I looked down and traced a circle around a rock with my big toe, hoping she wouldn't notice my watery eyes.

Joy put her hand on my shoulder. "Honey, I told Corinne that story, many years ago, almost in this same spot."

Air rushed out of me at the mention of my mother's name. I whipped my head up to face her. "You knew my mother?"

Her face softened. "I sure did." She stopped for a moment. "She was around here a lot in the old days, and we got to know each other, on account of us both liking to walk the beach."

I stared at her, a million questions surfacing in my mind.

But I didn't trust my voice to ask any of them. Joy started walking, and I went with her, pulled, like the tide to the moon. She turned to me and laughed softly. "You know, she learned all she knew about sea glass from me—from the best places to find it, to the rarest colors, to the story of the mermaids. She learned it from me, walking this same stretch of beach." I could only nod, willing her to go on. I ceased to be aware of the wind and cold and walked as if I was underwater. Joy's voice and the prospect of hearing more about my mother were the only things that filtered through. She looked over at me, and I saw sympathy and concern, the two hardest things in the world for me to take. "You look a lot like her, you know? Except for the brown eyes. That's your dad in you. Hers were the truest green I have ever seen. Sea green."

"That's what everyone says." I wiped my nose with my sweatshirt sleeve. "I wish I could really remember, on my own. We have a million pictures, but I feel like I don't have her in my mind without them. Just little bits, here and there." Joy squatted down to pick up a frosty white piece of glass, and we kept walking.

"You do, somewhere in there." We took a few steps in silence, and I wished that I believed her. "You know the clearest picture I have in my mind of her?" I raised my head, interested. "It was a day when we were walking around out here. She had come back for a visit, pregnant with you." She smiled. "She could barely bend over to pick anything up. All of a sudden she let out a scream, and I just about thought she was going into labor right here on the sand." I felt the lump in my throat recede. "I turned around, ready to holler for help, and saw her squatting down on the sand, arm stretched out behind her, like to steady herself."

"What was it?"

"Well, it wasn't labor that she was screamin' about. She had found herself a red piece of sea glass." A split-second image flashed in my mind. My mom letting me hold her red piece of glass, her telling me it was the rarest color. "It wasn't just a crumb, like I've found. It was a real beauty. She had a lucky eye that day." Joy's sunburned face creased as she smiled, and I saw her for someone genuine who had probably meant something to my mother.

"Hm." I brought my hand to the thin chain around my neck. "I have a piece of red. Did you ever hear of moonglass?"

"Can't say I have."

"Well, I think it's something we made up, my mom and me." I pulled out the red pendant and held it away from my neck. Joy stopped walking and let the glass rest in her hand, just beneath my chin.

"It's beautiful," she said, rubbing her thumb over the smooth surface. "No rough edges at all. Moonglass?" she asked, letting it fall to my sweatshirt.

"Yeah." I looked down at it. "When we lived up in Pismo and my dad worked nights, my mom and I would sometimes go for walks when there was a full moon and the tide was low. And one night I bent down to pick up what I thought was a rock, because I used to like to collect those, too, but it was a piece of sea glass. Since we were out at night, we called it moonglass."

"I've never thought to look for it at night," Joy said. "But that makes sense. A full moon brings the lowest tide, so that'd be the perfect time to look." She nodded at the necklace. "Was that the piece you found? Don't tell me you found a red piece of glass on the beach at night."

"No." I looked down at the sand. "Not that night. But it is

a piece of moonglass." I paused. "I found this one on another night. Just lying out in the middle of the wet sand, all by itself. The lights from the pier were shining off it." I moved it from side to side on the chain and looked down at the ground. "My dad had a hole drilled in it and made it into a necklace a while after. It's the one and only red piece I have."

Joy stooped down to pick up another green one, just as I saw it. "Well, honey, you keep that one close to you. That's a lucky treasure indeed. Probably was fresh from a mermaid on her way back out to sea." A wave of nausea washed over me just as the cool water rushed up over our feet. I shut my eyes for a moment, willing it away. When I opened them, a movement just in my peripheral vision made me turn.

It was the crawling man. He was just as I had seen him before, bent in a painful-looking bear crawl, head down, crosses swinging and pulling at his wrinkled neck. Joy noticed me looking and shook her head sympathetically.

"Never misses a Sunday. It could be pouring rain with waves thundering down onto the beach and hurricane winds, and he'll be out here, as predictable as the moon or tides. Every Sunday."

He didn't acknowledge us as he passed by but kept on his slow, methodical pace with resolve. I tilted my head to try to get a glimpse of his face, but it was shadowed except for the silver stubble on his chin. "Have you ever talked to him?"

Joy chewed her lip and continued to watch him. "No. He doesn't talk to anyone. I figure he doesn't think he deserves to. See that? His shirt?" I nodded. The single word stood out, bold and black in the wind. REPENT. "He blames himself for something, and in his mind there's no other way that he can make up for it besides reminding himself. And this is how he does it." We both watched him. "Everyone has their cross to bear, but his are right out there for us all to see. It's his guilt, strung around his neck."

I didn't say anything, suddenly aware of the weight of the red sea glass around my own neck.

"I've thought of talking to him," Joy went on. "Thought, all he needs is someone to tell it to, whatever it is. Let him get it off his chest so he can move on."

I stood, silent, watching the crawling man make his way, slowly, painfully, up the beach, doing his penance for something only he knew about. I knew the feeling. Nausea rolled hard through my stomach, and I turned away from Joy and dry-heaved over the sand. I felt a warm hand on my back as I stared hard at the sand in front of me.

"You better be getting back to your house. Tell your dad I said hello. And be good to him."

I stood up and wiped my mouth. "What do you mean?"

She looked down the beach toward our cottage, then back at me. "What I mean is, it can't be easy for him to be back here. I could see it all over him the other day. So give him some time."

I looked at her in disbelief. I'd appreciated a story about my mom, but this was overstepping. She had no idea. And no place.

"Well, thanks," I said curtly. "Thanks for enlightening me. I'll give my dad your regards." I turned and walked hard, wind at my back. As I did, a twinge of guilt worked its way around me like a corkscrew, but I didn't slow down.

11

A woman's laughter, followed by a familiar male voice, drifted down the steps from the backyard as I approached. I stopped midstep and listened, wavering between being peeved that someone was at the house and grateful for a distraction. And then I recognized a voice I had known since childhood.

"Holy shit!" Andy blurted out as I paused on the top step. "She jumped from the *top* of it? Dude . . ." My dad just shook his head and swallowed a hard swig of beer.

I leaned casually on the corner of the house and tried not to smile, proud that Andy seemed impressed. He saw me. "Anna Banana! We were just talking about you." He strode over and lifted me up, squeezing until I felt my headache returning. "Guess you had some night last night. Huh, kiddo? Chip off the old block! You know, back in the day your dad—"

My dad cut in. "I think she got her little dose of history last night." He glanced at me and offered a tentative smile. A smile that asked if we could drop it for now. I looked away. "Besides, you were supposed to back me up and tell her how dangerous that jump is. And with lifeguards, too."

Andy put on a stern look and raised his index finger at me. "No sixteen-year-old girl should be jumping off rocks, drunk, in the middle of the night. With *lifeguards*. How's that?"

Judging by their tone, they weren't on their first beers. The mood felt genuinely light with them together, and I was too tired to stay mad. I raised an eyebrow. "Just so you have the story right, I wasn't drunk. And I think it was only midnight or so. And I thought you were always supposed to swim near a lifeguard. But you're well on your way to being a strict disciplinarian. "

My dad took another swig and rolled his eyes. Andy held up his beer, tipping his head. "Well said. Joey, I think the girl can hold her own. Anna, don't go jumping off any more rocks. You'll give your old man a heart attack. Now. Let's call it done and get out there."

He looked from me to my dad, who I could tell was almost ready to let it go. He probably thought he should make me sweat it, so I obliged and walked over to him, doing my best to look remorseful. "Dad . . . I'm sorry I jumped off the rock that you made legendary. I was just trying to make you proud." I gave a little shrug and looked down, knowing it had a pretty good chance of working, since Andy was there.

He tried to keep a straight face for a second, then shook his head and turned, trying to hide a smile. "You smart-ass. You're lucky I didn't drag the rest of the underaged off the beach too. That woulda made you a real hit with everyone." I silently thanked God or fate or whatever that he hadn't.

"Who's a hit?"

I turned around at the sound of the female voice and saw, coming out of the kitchen carrying a glass of wine, a woman that had to be Andy's. She was exactly what he liked. Tall, blond, big boobs—fake—and tan—also fake. She was definitely enough to match his tall swimmer physique. I bet she had fallen for that and the wavy hair. She stepped gingerly over the uneven paver stones of the patio and stopped in front of me.

"You must be Anna. Well, *you* are gorgeous. Remind me not to stand next to you for too long." She looked over at Andy, waiting for him to introduce her.

He abruptly clunked down his beer and walked over to us, stifling a burp. "Anna, this is Tamra."

I smiled politely and stuck out my hand. "Nice to meet you. So . . . you're Andy's new girlfriend?"

Andy coughed. Tamra clutched her wine. My dad glanced over at me, and I knew I shouldn't have said "new." Andy was always in search of the love of his life, and he met them over and over. His string of girlfriends stretched long over the years that he had come to visit us. Every time, it was a new one. That was just how I thought of them.

Andy regained his composure, wrapped his arm around Tamra's shoulder, and grinned. "Yeah, sure. I thought you two ladies could get to know each other while we dive. Tamra has lived here in Newport Beach her whole life and went to Coast High. I thought she could fill you in on school and shopping and all that stuff, you know?" Tamra had smoothed her face over and now wore a polite smile that I guessed she had perfected a long time ago. Even my dad looked a bit hopeful.

I bit my bottom lip, trying not to smile. Just as Andy thought it was highly important to have women in his life, he also seemed to think that I needed them, as role models or something. Never mind that they were almost interchangeable. His intentions were mostly good, but I also figured it was because he wanted someone to take the women off his hands every so often so he could still hang out with my dad. I looked at him, falsely sweet. "Oh, that's so nice. But, um, I think I'm actually gonna dive with you guys. " I looked back at Tamra in her tight dress and heels. "You should come. I have an extra wet suit."

She shivered a little, then let out a laugh as if I had suggested something ridiculous, which I had. "Honey, I'll be up here in that living room of yours with my glass of wine and *Cosmo*, waiting for some fresh fish." She nudged Andy. "You said you'd get me a halibut, right?"

He nodded confidently. "Sunday Poke-N-Eat, baby." She looked puzzled. He grabbed up a three-pronged pole spear and jabbed at the air. "You know, poke . . . and eat. Old cove tradition, back from the good ol' days when we all—"

"Hey, catch!" My dad threw Andy's wet suit at him and then walked over to the shed and started pulling out our collection of dive gear. Tamra smacked Andy on the butt and then disappeared back through the kitchen door. I looked out at the choppy water, not entirely sure I wanted to go diving, but sure enough that I didn't want to spend the rest of the afternoon making small talk with Barbie incarnate.

I fished my wet suit out of the pile that had been thrown out of the rubber tub, and started turning it right side out. It was completely dried out and stiff with salt from whenever I had gone out last, so putting it on involved a mix of pulling and hopping and cursing under my breath. Once I was zipped in, I pulled the hood over my head and tried to adjust to the squished cheeks it gave me. My dream was to be able to dive with no wet suit, but I had yet to make it to water warm enough for that, so next I put on gloves and then grabbed my fins and mask and followed the guys down to the water.

We made a silly-looking procession that drew the looks of a couple of kids playing in the late-afternoon glow near the waterline. My dad carried his spear gun and a take bag and looked like serious business. Andy followed him, dragging his pole spear behind. I had shot my dad's spear gun before and liked the muted *thunk* it made when I pulled the trigger underwater, but I didn't have any interest in shooting fish. I just liked to be out there and getting a look at the things most people never did.

The wind had died down almost completely, and I stood at the water's edge watching the remaining choppiness roll with each swell. My dad walked back to me and spit into his mask, then rubbed it around. "We're going to work the rocks just beyond the tide pools and go south a ways. Try your best to stay near us." He smiled and pulled his mask down over his eyes, leaving the snorkel hanging off to the side. "If you get separated or get spooked or something, you know which way the shore is. You're gonna love it out there. It's gorgeous."

I nodded and spit into my own mask, then used my thumbs to rub it around. I could see Andy's head out beyond the surf line already. My dad waited while I put on my mask, and we walked out together into waist-deep water, pausing to put on our fins before we submerged our faces into the choppy water.

The surface water was still all stirred up from the wind, so at first I saw only tiny particles suspended in hazy blue, and the bubbles that came up from my dad's fins kicking in front of me. We kicked straight out and then made a turn so we were parallel to the shore, headed for the outer rocks of the tide pools. The only sounds I was aware of were my own rhythmic breathing, exaggerated through my snorkel, and the occasional gurgle of air bubbles rising to the surface. The rest was a kind of quiet that only existed underwater. I settled into it, brought my arms down against my sides, and scanned the water below me.

We came to an area of rock covered in eel grass that promised a bit more clarity. My dad stopped ahead of me and let his legs sink down below him so that he hovered, vertical. He was watching something. I saw nothing but the grass that waved and rolled languidly with each swell, like a woman's long hair. He stayed still a second longer and then shook his head and began to kick again. Directly below me a bright orange Garibaldi darted out from under a rock overhang and swam right under me like I was invisible. That wouldn't have been what my dad was looking for, and I wondered for a second what else he had seen.

I floated there, watching the grass slip back and forth with the swell, and I caught a glimpse of what looked like it could be an abalone shell, about the size of my head, clinging to the rocks below. I took a deep breath through my snorkel, then pointed my head straight down at the bottom, kicking hard above me with my fins. Diving down, I was aware of two things: the almost immediate pressure in my ears, and how much light I lost in just a few feet of water. I plugged my nose and blew gently, releasing the pressure. It wasn't far down, maybe ten feet or so, but it was noticeably darker. And cooler. I grabbed a handful of eel grass in each of my hands and moved along the pitted surface of the rock as far as my anchors would let me. The dim light made it hard to see the bright colors that I knew were there, but I was able to make out the small, curling fronds of a cluster of Spanish shawls, tiny plants that would wave bright purple and orange in better diving conditions. Just as I found the abalone again, my lungs started the burn that I knew meant I only had another few seconds before I'd have to surface and take another breath. I ran my gloved hand over the bumpy surface of the massive abalone and tugged just a bit to see if there was any give.

As I did, I caught a flash of what looked like blond hair moving by the periphery of my mask. I startled and kicked hard for the surface. Above me, I could see weak daylight, waving and distorted. It didn't take more than a few kicks before I broke through and blew hard to clear my snorkel. I lifted my mask to my forehead and looked around the now calm surface of the water, and then below me, my heart rate slowing. Then I saw it on my shoulder and had to laugh, though the laugh wasn't absent of nervousness. My ponytail had somehow snuck its way out of my hood and was now trailing over my shoulder and down my arm.

All of Joy's mermaid talk had me a little spooked. Stupid. I took a deep breath and scanned the surface of the water for some sign of the guys—bubbles or fins or something. They were nowhere to be seen. The sun was now almost touching the silhouette of Catalina, and I figured there was less than a half hour of good light left, so without completely deciding to go in, I put my mask in the water and kicked with slow, exaggerated kicks back over the rocks and headed to our original path. There wasn't much to see in the haziness, and for the first time in a long time, I didn't feel completely at ease in the water. Something had shifted in me, and as much as I tried to shake it off, I couldn't help but sweep my mask back and forth as I swam, checking to make sure that nothing was following me.

Beneath me, on the bottom, a dark band of small rocks and bits of shell came into view and moved millimeters back and forth with the swell. On a low tide this would be a good spot to look for sea glass. Now it was too dark, and starting to feel too cold. I popped my head up and found that I had made it back to the water directly in front of our house. In the light of the living room window, I could see Tamra in my green chair, wineglass in hand, looking out in my direction. To the right of our house, my mother's cottage stood shadowed except for one last corner of sunlight glinting on the dusty upstairs window. For a moment I tried to picture her on the balcony, golden and warm, but I couldn't see her. I put my head back down and kicked in.

I got out of my dive gear as quietly and slowly as humanly possible, hoping to buy enough time for the guys to show up so I wouldn't have to make small talk with Tamra. I still felt a little bad about the "new girlfriend" comment. I also didn't really have anything to say to her that wouldn't sound totally forced, so I was hoping for a buffer. No such luck. I snuck in through the back door and locked myself in the bathroom.

Steam rose up in curls around me, and I closed my eyes and stuck my face directly into the hot streams of water. I felt a mild regret for not sticking it out and staying with my dad. We'd spent countless summer days swimming around in the ocean together exploring, and when we finally dragged ourselves up onto the sand, sunburned and noodle-armed, he couldn't have been happier. *We* couldn't have been happier. It had always been our way of being close without having to talk about it, and for a while it had suited us both. But that closeness felt like it was slipping away, separated now by the spaces between what we said to each other. I finished washing the smell of salt and wet suit from me and shut off the shower, resolving to try to talk to him about it. Somehow.

When I shut off the water, I expected to hear the voices of the guys, just in from the water, but they weren't there yet. There was no avoiding Tamra at this point. I walked out to the living room, towel wrapped around my head, and found her looking at a black-and-white picture of my mother and me. In it my mom stood in her bathing suit and a big floppy hat, holding me above her head, my tiny legs stretched out behind me like I was flying. My dad must have snapped it at the perfect moment, because although her eyes are hidden under the shadow of the hat, her mouth is open and smiling, like she's laughing or talking to me as she swings me high in the air.

Tamra turned, sincere concern on her face. "You must miss her, huh?"

I shrugged, but didn't move my eyes from the picture, so she looked back at it too. "I guess so," I said casually. "She's been gone a long time, since I was seven, so it's just how things have been for a long time. I'm used to it."

She swirled her wineglass a tiny bit, then took a sip and turned to me again.

"Yeah, but, *honey*, you're coming up on a time in life when you are gonna *need* another woman, a mom, to guide you through all the craziness." Her voice broke off at the end, and she sniffed.

I looked at her more closely, realizing with amusement that she had actually gotten teary. She sniffed again, then finished off the last of the wine in her glass, which was probably the last of the bottle, if I had to guess. She walked over to the window, empty glass in hand, looking forlornly at the water. I breathed in deeply through my nose and pressed my lips together to keep from smiling, then walked over to stand next to her. This wasn't the reaction I was used to.

In the twilight I could see one of the guys, probably my dad, walking up from the water with a large fish in tow. Andy's dark head bobbed in the water beyond him. Tamra was still sniffing and looking pitiful, so I put my hand on her back and patted. "We're fine, my dad and me. Honestly, we're good. And if I need a woman to talk to, I can always get a hold of you through Andy, right?"

She smiled, then turned and pulled me into a hug, which was awkward for a few reasons, two of which pressed hard like rocks into my own chest. She pulled back and held me by my shoulders, breathing sweet wine breath on me. "Good. You call me anytime. Prom, dating, birth control, whatever."

Just when it couldn't get any more awkward, I heard the back door to the kitchen open up. My dad's voice came through, obviously happy at what he'd brought in. "Hey, Anna? Could you grab me my fillet knife? I gotta get this guy ready to throw on the grill. Fish tacos tonight!"

I pried myself from Tamra's arms, and she went to fix her face. Out the window the sun had disappeared completely, leaving the last hint of a glow behind Catalina. I thought of Joy and the mermaid tears, the Crawler and my moonglass, my mother having lived yards away from where I stood. Joy had been right about stories making things more beautiful. I watched the gray surface of the water roll with the swells, and I came up with a new story. I told myself that maybe the years she was with us were like when the full moon shone for the mermaids, when they could walk on land and be with the ones they loved. And that maybe, like them, she'd had no choice but to go back.

I dive deeply into crystal blue water. I don't wear a mask or snorkel or fins or a wet suit. I don't need to. I belong here, below the surface. All around me the ocean is radiant with life. Bright blue fish dart in and out of giant coral fans, and towering columns of kelp wave gently as I weave my way through them. The water is far too deep for me to see the bottom, but below me what looks like a tiny spark at first begins to expand into an eerie glow. Suddenly the water around me grows cooler and I want only to be in the warmth of the glow, so I angle my body downward and kick. The farther down I go, the more I need to find the source of light and warmth, so I kick harder, propelling myself into what should be cold, dark water.

And then I see her, and I stop dead, suspended in the liquid stillness of the water.

The mermaid's long blond hair flows and curls around the luminous curves of her body as she swims, inches above the sparkling ocean floor. I stay still, afraid that if I move, she'll disappear. Her movements are fluid and strong as she hovers over the sand, pausing briefly at a large rock before moving on. Without thinking about it, I know she's searching for something, though I'm not sure what it is. I want to help her find it, so I bring my feet together and give a tentative kick, disturbing the stillness of the water.

She freezes, startled, then turns and fixes her sad green eyes on me. Her face is distressed at first, but softens when our eyes meet. There is a pang in my chest, somewhere between deep sorrow and shining hope.

My mother.

And then, as if the same realization hits her, she shoots upward, toward the surface, leaving me behind in a dark whirl of tiny bubbles.

I am paralyzed at the bottom of the ocean as the last of the bubbles swirl up and then disappear into the blue above me. I sink down onto the sand, alone and suddenly cold. I am there only a moment before I have the sensation that it is raining underwater. Something lands beside my foot, creating a tiny, momentary puff of sand.

I lift my chin slowly, and the coldness that I feel gives way to silent wonder. All around me gleaming drops of color make their way down through the fluid smoothness. They move in slow motion, spiraling down, catching and throwing light as they descend. I reach out my hand to catch a cobalt drop, and as it slips between my fingers, I recognize its smooth, solid surface.

At that moment I am conscious of the sound that I somehow know has been there all along. As it gains strength, the ocean floor explodes with tiny puffs of sand, drops of sea glass settling down into it.

Above me, my mother is weeping.

12

I didn't go near the water for nearly a week. Instead I left in the morning for practice, where I ran hard enough that Jillian had a hard time sticking with me, and Coach Martin reminded me repeatedly to save my legs for the upcoming meet. After practice I went to the shopping center across the highway and aimlessly wandered the stores, even when I could tell that the shopgirls were completely irritated. I spent hours on end at the Starbucks, listening from behind my magazine to people order, and talk on their cell phones, and gossip. I came home after dark, so I didn't have to look at my mom's cottage or decline my dad's invitations to surf before he had to go to work.

On the weekend, when we finally passed in the hall, Dad paused and grabbed me gently by the shoulders. "Hey, stranger! Haven't seen much of you since I switched over to nights. Feels like I'm living with a ghost." He looked me over carefully. "Everything okay, kiddo?"

I shrugged his hands off. "I know. Sorry. I'm just busy with practice, and school starts tomorrow, so I wanted to do a little shopping . . ."

His mouth fell open. "Oh, jeez. I'm sorry, hon. I didn't realize it was tomorrow." He pulled out his wallet and handed me a crisp hundred-dollar bill. "Here. Why don't you go out with Ashley or something and pick yourself up a few new things for school then?"

I didn't answer at first. I hadn't actually meant I wanted to go shopping.

"You know . . . here. Use this instead." He took back the hundred and handed me his ATM card. "Just in case you need a little more. You know the PIN."

I twirled the card slowly between my fingers before tucking it into my pocket. "Thanks, Dad, but you don't need to give me this."

He laid a heavy hand on my head. "Hey. I realize it's not easy starting out someplace new. But you're gonna be fine. Don't sweat it."

"I know, I know. Thank you." I forced a smile he could believe, then turned to go before he could see it slip away.

"Have fun," he called after me. "Go big if you want—it's your one chance. This promotion's gotta be good for something."

I sat on the edge of a fountain that shot water high up into the air in predictable rhythmic intervals. Each time it did, two little girls who were hanging over the edge of it screamed with delight as mist fell over them. Their mom sat a few feet away, texting, and shushed them without looking up. At least they had each other.

The mist felt good on my skin in the heat of the day, and I tried to soak it up. When I'd gotten to the mall, Dad's ATM card in hand, I'd perked up a bit. He'd never just handed it over like that. Definitely not with instructions to "go big." Either he was feeling guilty or his promotion really was worth something. Whatever it was, the little mood lift it gave me faded when I couldn't get ahold of Ashley and had to go shopping by myself. I thought of Shelby and Laura and how we would have made a day of it. We would've passed clothes back and forth over the dressing room walls, stepped out to show each outfit, critiquing all the while, and talked each other into the things we loved and wanted to borrow later on. Then we would have sat here together at this fountain with coffee drinks or ice cream cones, dissecting what the first day of school would be like—which teachers we'd end up with, who'd be completely changed over the summer, and where we'd be having lunch. As it was, I'd half heartedly picked a few sundresses off a surf store sale rack and grabbed a new pair of sandals without even trying them on, and now I sat staring at the center of the fountain, feeling pitifully alone.

"Hey, Anna."

I looked up to see Jillian standing with a woman who had to be her mom. They stood next to each other, smoothie cups in hand, almost mirror images with the same slender build, long legs, and brown eyes. Her mom stepped forward, smiling. "I'm Beth, Jilly's mom. And you must be the Anna that Jill's been talking about. You girls should do pretty well this season, from what I hear."

I smiled back, heartened a little by her immediate warmth

and the fact that Jillian had mentioned me to her mom. I tried to match her cheery tone. "Hopefully. I've never competed before, so we'll see."

Jillian raised an eyebrow, smiling. "I thought we competed every day at practice. You've been kicking my butt the last three days."

Beth leaned into me a little, her voice a half-whisper. "Good job. Keep it up. She needs a good training partner, someone to push her every now and then." Jillian gave her a look, and Beth put a hand on each of our shoulders. "Anna, it is so good to meet you. I can't wait to see you race. Jilly, hon, I need to run into the bookstore. Meet you back here in a few minutes?"

She nodded without looking at her mom. "See you in a few."

Beth gave one more wave before she turned and headed down the cobblestone row of stores, and I watched until I couldn't see her anymore. "Your mom's really nice."

"She's superhappy I'm running again—which I get, but she can be a little much sometimes." Jillian sat next to me on the edge of the fountain, and I wondered if the "again" had something to do with her sister. She motioned to my bag. "Anyway. Last-minute school shopping?"

"Kind of. If you count sale rack sundresses. I'm not too into shopping. Or school starting."

Jillian took a sip of her smoothie. "That why you've been running all crazy this week? Are you stressed out about it or something?"

Even she'd noticed. I watched a stream of water fly up and then separate into little droplets before raining back down. "I guess so."

She shrugged. "Don't worry about it. You have the team

already." She grinned and bumped my shoulder. "And you have Ashley, too."

I nodded, surprised at how good it felt to have someone other than my dad reassure me. "That's true. What more do I need, really?"

"You need to know two things—" Jillian's phone chimed with a text. She glanced at her purse. "God, she's quick, my mom." Jillian grabbed her cup and stood. "I gotta go meet her."

"Wait—what are the two things?" I really wanted to know.

"Oh. The first one is that tomorrow will look like a ridiculous fashion show, but nobody keeps that up past the first week. The second thing is . . . our school is small, and people will know you're new so just be ready to feel like they're sizing you up. Because they are."

The flip-flop my stomach did must have shown on my face. Jillian put her hand on my shoulder. "I didn't tell you to make you nervous. Don't be. I told you so you can walk in there well prepared." I started to ask her what she meant, but she'd already turned to go. "See you tomorrow! Hold your head high!"

Hold my head high? What was that supposed to mean? I didn't have anything to be ashamed of. I didn't think.

Great.

13

Jillian was right about the whole fashion show thing. Immaculately dressed people funneled into the courtyard, all tanned and beautiful and looking like they'd stepped out of a magazine. I looked down at my schedule and then back up, hoping to see Jillian or Ashley among them. All around me were groups I didn't belong to. The guys stood around in clothes far more expensive than mine and nodded while making small talk and eyeing the girls. The girls, on the other hand, paraded in, all in carefully chosen outfits that had probably been weeks in the making. When they saw each other, they squealed and rushed to meet, chat, compliment, and then size up everyone else. Which made me thankful for Jillian's warning. I didn't want to be the topic of anyone's conversation, so I tried to blend in. Clearly, though, I didn't.

I hadn't given what I would be wearing much thought until

that morning. It was still warm even early in the morning, so I had pulled out one of my new sundresses, clipped the tag off, slid into my flip-flops, and finger-combed out my hair, letting it hang loose and wavy down my back. I was fine with what I was wearing; it was just the standing alone, awkwardly checking and rechecking my schedule that made me feel out of place. I needed something else to look at.

As if my thoughts were broadcast over the intercom, Tyler walked into the far end of the courtyard, up to another lifeguard I recognized from the party, and high-fived him. They exchanged a few words, then both turned to take in the mass of people milling around. I was about to look away and pretend I hadn't seen him, when his eyes met mine for a brief instant. He didn't outwardly acknowledge me, but the hint of a smile crossed his face as he scanned the remainder of the courtyard, looking like he owned the place. I checked my schedule again. Algebra II, room 101, Mr. Strickland.

"Heeyy!" A pink fruity-smelling blur of blond hair and tan skin ran up and hugged me. "You look SO cute! I love the beach-casual. Have you been here long? Sorry I'm late—I had a minor clothes crisis this morning." I just nodded, sure that she'd launch into the full story of it. Instead she jumped right to a new topic.

"Oh! So how much trouble were you in for the other night? You should have seen your dad when he got ·there. It was so scary. I thought I was gonna get arrested for bringing the champagne. And then later when Tyler swam in, *he* was all freaked out about it, and—" As she said it, I saw Tyler heading in our direction, and I immediately whipped up my schedule.

"Hey, Ash. Do you have lip gloss?"

She glanced at Tyler, immediately getting it, and handed

me the tube. Then she tilted her head in, whispering, "So, what happened between you guys out at that rock? He seemed superworried when he came in. Like, maybe he-kinda-likes-you worried." She smiled and nudged me with her shoulder.

I took another quick glance as he came our way, looking beyond us like he wasn't gonna stop. "No," I said definitively. "He doesn't like me. He's just scared to death of my dad, that's all."

Tyler approached us, not bothering to hide the smirk that now played across his face. "Little Ryan. . . . Whitmore. Glad to see you're both alive and well." He nodded to each of us.

That greeting reiterated what I had just told Ashley, though I hadn't really believed it when I'd said it. I was immediately annoyed.

"Morning!" Ashley practically sang.

I shifted my weight and smiled thinly. "Hey." Nothing else came to mind. Nothing that I could say out loud, at least. I had only ever seen Tyler in his trunks on the beach, and he had looked like every other lifeguard around. And like that, there had been a possibility between us. Here at school it was obvious that he probably came from the same kind of money as everyone else. He was dressed casually, in jeans and a T-shirt and flip-flops of his own, but the giveaway was in the way he carried himself. Totally relaxed and sure. Like he belonged here.

The bell rang, and Ashley squeezed my arm. "Hey! I gotta go. I have dance yoga first period." Tyler was looking at her with an amused expression, and I had to smile. "Meet me out here at lunch, okay?" she continued. "We don't want to have to do the whole new-girl/walk-the-quad-and-try-to-figure-out-where-to-sit thing." I opened my mouth to respond, but didn't get the chance. She eyed Tyler for a second. "Unless you have other plans already."

I jumped in quickly this time, trying to avoid an awkward moment. "No. I'll meet you."

"Okay, good! I brought you lunch too, so you don't have to eat the cafeteria food before practice today." She started to bounce away, then turned around. "Good luck!"

"Thanks."

Tyler took a step closer. My cheeks burned as I fought the urge to take a step backward. He smelled so good. "You've got quite the little caretaker there." He glanced down at my schedule. "Where you headed first?"

I looked at the now crinkled paper in my hand, which was ridiculous, because I had my schedule memorized at this point. "Math, in 101. Mr. Strickland?"

He raised his eyebrows and smirked. "Oh, you're in for a real treat. The guy's a total hard-ass. Fails half his class every year, which is why I won't be the only senior in there."

"You're in there too?" I asked, trying to sound only mildly interested. "First?"

"Yeah. We better get going. He's gonna make an example of somebody today, and you don't want it to be you."

Upstairs we filed into room 101 with a line of other students who chattered and compared schedules. A short man in a cowboy hat stood with his back to the class, writing frenetically on the whiteboard. I looked around for an empty seat, preferably near the back. Tyler had already found a desk a couple of rows over and had his hand on the one behind it. He motioned to me to hurry up, so I weaved my way over and slid into the chair behind him. Right on cue with the final bell, Mr. Strickland turned around and leveled his eyes on a girl who was still leaning on her desk, rummaging through her purse.

"Does your mama let you sit in your mashed potatoes at home?" he bellowed through a thick mustache. The girl looked confused, but then plunked down in her chair and looked at her lap.

Mr. Strickland scanned the room for another victim. I scanned the walls behind his desk, which were covered with different notes and drawings tacked up haphazardly. A wooden paddle with holes drilled into it hung above them all, the handle emblazoned with a carved silhouette that resembled Yosemite Sam and Mr. Strickland at the same time. He saw me looking and turned his attention on me. "You must be Joe Ryan's daughter." I flinched, then shifted in my seat, getting ready for whatever saying he was going to spit at me, but it didn't come. "Smart guy, your old man. Hopefully he passed it on." I nodded once, silent. He looked down his roll sheet until he found me. "Louanna Ryan." Tyler cleared his throat loudly and shifted in his seat in front of me.

I fought the urge to roll my eyes or kick his desk. "Just Anna, please."

Mr. Strickland looked at me a quick second, then fixed his eyes on Tyler. "Evans! You sick or something? I am. Sick of you already." Tyler shrugged, but didn't say anything. Mr. Strickland looked back at me, a little softer. "Well, Ms. Ryan, the thing you need to know about this class, as lots of people in here can tell you from previous experience, is that God helps those who help themselves, so if you don't get it, get off your lazy you-know-what and help yourself." We were all silent, and I waited for a translation, explanation, something.

"I'm in here every morning, six a.m. if you need help, so no one has any excuse not to pass my class." I looked around at the other glazed-looking faces and wondered how many of them were repeaters. "Now get out your books. Let's get started. First test is next Friday."

Tyler leaned back in his desk and turned his head just enough for me to see the smirk that had now become familiar. "Told you . . . Louanna."

"Yeah, he seems like a real fan of yours," I whispered, leaning forward.

Strickland stopped writing and turned slowly from the whiteboard. "Evans. Didn't your mama teach you it's not polite to talk while I'm giving you the most important formula you'll need in this class?"

I looked at the board studiously, then back at my paper, trying not to crack a smile. Instruction resumed, and in front of me Tyler shook his head.

The rest of the day until lunch went by uneventfully. My other teachers were young and enthusiastic. All assured us that this year what we were going to learn would be exciting and relevant to our lives. All were happy to make a little note on their roll sheet to call me Anna. And none of them had known either one of my parents. By the time I got to lunch, I was feeling a tiny bit optimistic that school here might not be so bad. I was even starting to feel thankful that I had somewhere to go during the day, away from the beach and all of the things I didn't want to think about there.

As soon as the lunch bell rang, my phone vibrated with a text from Ashley. "Lunch on south green. Lots 2 tell u!" I looked at the map on the back of my schedule and headed down a steep path that overlooked the small upscale-artsy town and the ocean beyond. On the sides of the path were stone tables sheltered by umbrellas. Ashley sat at a sunny one, arranging an array of small plastic containers. Then she folded her hands and looked around, barely able to hold still. When she saw me, she waved excitedly.

"Hey! Come, sit!" I made my way over and set my bag down, eyeing the lunch spread, which looked like it had come from a gourmet deli. "Grab a sandwich and some fruit. That's your best bet for before practice today. I just read it in *Runner's World*. You know, slow-release energy, because I talked to Coach Martin and you guys have a long run today."

I reached for the paper-wrapped sandwich. "Thanks. So, what, you're his assistant now or something?"

She handed me a bottle of water and opened up one for herself, then turned to face me. "Sort of. Anyway, what do you think so far? How's your first day?"

I swallowed a mouthful of sandwich and nodded, trying to match her enthusiasm. "It's good. My first-period teacher is a little old-school, and seems to have it out for Tyler, but other than that it's good."

"Tyler's in first with you?" Her eyes widened. "That's great, right? Maybe he can 'tutor' you." She notched quotation marks in the air.

I took a swig of water. "I don't think so. It's his second time in there. And anyway, he's not interested. I can tell."

Ashley's hand flew to her mouth, and I thought she had bit her tongue or something. "That's even better! You could tutor him! It's perfect!" She clapped her hands together, and when she did, I noticed she had had her nails done pink with tiny flowers painted on them to match her outfit.

"I don't think I'm his type. He's probably got a zillion girls here after him."

Ashley looked at me very matter-of-factly. "Oh, he does. He's Tyler Evans. But . . ." She leaned in close and lowered her voice, despite the fact that there was no one else around. "That's what I had to tell you! Everybody is talking about you. And him. They're saying you two left everyone else in the water and hooked up out there. They're also saying you were drunk and naked." She took a dainty bite of her sandwich.

I choked on a gulp at the back of my throat. "What? None of that is true. You were there . . ."

"I know, I know. Whoever started that last one was jealous. Because you supposedly hooked up with the most sought-after senior, which is what these two girls in my first-period class told me Tyler is. They saw us all standing together this morning and were totally asking me about you. Not in a bitchy way or anything, though, don't worry." I shook my head, slightly amazed that Jillian had nailed it so well.

"Anyway," Ashley was saying, "I know I was the one who talked you into running, but would you *hate* me if I quit? The girls I met in first said that if I do dance, it counts for PE, and I never really liked getting all sweaty running. Plus, dance clothes are way more flattering on me than running clothes."

I gave her an are-you-kidding-me look, but really I didn't mind too much. She hadn't actually run at the last few practices anyway, and I'd felt like I should hang out with her even though I would have liked to talk to Jillian more. "That's fine, Ash. I think I'm gonna stick with it, though. I kinda like getting all sweaty."

"I know. I could tell that about you when we met. Hey," she

said, suddenly serious, "it doesn't mean we'll stop hanging out or anything."

"No, no, of course not." I smiled at her. Most likely we'd find our own circles of people we fit in with. That was just the way it worked. But she'd grown on me, and I already considered her a friend.

She looked at her watch and pushed a small, dense lump that resembled a cookie at me. "Eat this right after seventh. It's a little energy nugget. I saw the recipe in some health food book and gave it to our chef. Hopefully it's edible."

I took the nugget. "Thanks. And thanks for lunch, Ash." I slipped my backpack over my shoulders, and she grabbed up her giant black bag. "I appreciate it—everything, I mean."

She tilted her head and smiled, then gave me a quick hug. "It's what I do." And then she was bouncing off again. I checked the room number for my seventh-period class and headed toward the three-hundred building.

14

The tardy bell rang, and I slid into my seat, grateful that last period had finally arrived. Despite the fact that there was no teacher in the front of the room, the chatter that came in from the hallway had dwindled to a whisper here and there as everyone looked around for some direction. I saw a blond girl from my math class, but when we made eye contact, she looked away quickly without acknowledging me. Someone cleared their throat from the back of the room, and the distinct clack of heels slowly made its way up one of the rows.

"Well, good afternoon. Aren't you all just a bundle of energy today." Everyone else turned back to look, but I recognized her voice from the beach immediately and kept my eyes straight ahead, focused hard on the whiteboard. This had to be a joke. No wonder she could quote poetry. Her heels clacked up the aisle in slow, measured steps, and I wondered if her feet ached after a summer of barefoot walks on the beach. I snuck a look once she passed my row. With her hair pulled back into a bun and her tailored dress, I might not have even recognized her at first. The only hint of the Joy from the beach was the tanned skin that crinkled around her eyes as she turned around and smiled warmly at us. I looked down immediately.

"Welcome," she said. Nobody said anything. Out of the corner of my eye, I saw a few heads nod. "Well"—she straightened up—"I'm sure you've spent the day listening to everyone's class rules and plans, and that you probably didn't *really* listen to any of it. It's your first day back, I know. Mine too. I'm Ms. Lewis." *Joy Lewis,* I thought. Who knew my mother, and too much about me to be my teacher. *Perfect.*

She spoke in a calm but firm voice. "My rules are simple. I expect you to act like responsible people." She paused, and I looked out the window, which framed blue sky and the barely discernable horizon of the ocean. "And I expect you to think."

I glanced up. She was at the front of the classroom, scanning our faces for some flicker of something. I watched her eyes look up and down the rows, until they stopped at me, and this time I didn't look away. There was a visible shift in her expression and a noticeable beat before she spoke again, like she had lost the thread of her speech. She smiled vaguely and nodded before continuing.

"Since this is World Literature, we'll be starting at the beginning, with a favorite topic of mine. Mythology." *Of course.* I looked down at my desk, but I could feel her eyes still on me. "Now, I don't mean your standard Greek mythology. You guys did that in seventh grade. This quarter we're gonna take a look at some lesser-known myths. Some that have found their way into our movies and books and music without us even realizing what they are." She looked around, and we sat in silence. I focused hard on the letters carved into the corner of the desk. Thick layers of blue and black ink spelled out a four-letter word that echoed my general sentiment at the moment.

She chuckled softly. "You guys are a tough audience, this first day of school, last class of the day. I get it. I'd rather be out there too, to tell you the truth." She motioned to the window and finally won a few murmurs of agreement. "How about this. Anyone have an idea about why we have myths in the first place?"

After a long moment a brunette in the front row raised her hand and spoke tentatively. "Um, to explain things people didn't understand?"

Joy (Ms. Lewis) clapped her hands, and I glanced up. "Yes, honey! *Thank you!* To explain the things we don't understand. Because it's *in* us to want to answer things, right? The things that nag at us and keep us up at night, wondering. It's human nature to want answers." I swore her eyes flicked to me for a second before she went on. "So that's where we'll start. With questions that need to be answered. Tomorrow. I'm gonna give you the rest of the period today to flip through your books, read the intro, and come up with a question you think people, as in humans, need answered. A big question. And I'll be willing to bet there's a myth that takes a crack at it."

Nobody moved.

"Go on now. Get your books and paper out and your brains going. It's time to start thinking."

Backpacks unzipped and papers rustled around me. I just sat there. It had felt like she was talking just to me the whole time, like she knew what I was thinking, and it had me almost frozen. There were things I'd thought I wanted answered for a long time, but I wasn't sure of them anymore. It seemed like the answers could be worse than the wondering. It was why I tiptoed around the topic of my mom just as much as my dad did. I'd yet to find out why he hadn't told me about her living at the cove, or when they left, or what their story was, but the unknown was frightening. Maybe it was something too hard for him to tell, that would put us back in the painful place we were in for so long after she was gone. Maybe it wasn't worth it to know. Maybe she could just stay a question, like the crawling man, a kind of myth of her own. My mother.

I pulled out my English notebook and opened it to the first page, which was still clean and blank. My pencil hovered over the center of the page. Around me, most people sat the same way, either flipping pages in the book or staring at blank notebook pages, unsure of how to proceed. For a teacher she'd left things pretty wide open. The seconds ticking away on the clock were now audible. Joy (I still couldn't think of her differently) walked softly to the first desk in my aisle, paused to look at the boy's notebook, then made her way down the row. When she got to my desk, she put a hand on my shoulder, but I stiffened and she took it away.

"No questions yet, huh?" I shook my head. "Well, give yourself some time. I'm sure you'll come up with a few." She took a step to leave, but then paused. "Why don't you stay after class a minute. I've got something for you."

For the rest of the period I yearned for and dreaded the bell. When it finally rang, I took in a deep breath and slowly packed up my stuff. The room cleared out, and I was left standing uncomfortably, backpack slung over one shoulder, ready to make a quick exit if need be.

Once everyone was gone, she walked over to a packed shelf

behind her desk and pulled a worn book out, flipping through it with a faint smile. "You may like this one. Your mother sure did. Said it inspired some of her paintings."

Paintings?

The question must have shown on my face.

"She was a brilliant artist, even at a young age. I think it was the way she tried to work things out for herself. We've all got something we do, and hers was painting." She nodded to herself. "I'm guessing your dad didn't save any of her work, then."

I had no memory of her painting. Ever. Never heard my dad mention it either. I stared down at the book she held out to me. Adorning the cover, in curling ornate lettering, was the title *Mermaids: Daughters of the Sea.*

I didn't say anything. She pushed it gently into my hands. "Take it. It's a place to start."

"Thanks," I managed, pushing it to the crook of my arm.

"Anna," she said softly, "answers to most of our questions do exist. You just have to ask them."

"Yeah," I said curtly. "I need to go. Um . . . thank you for this." I walked past her and out the door, sure of two things: One, I needed to change my English class, and two, I could run for miles today and not feel a thing.

"Long. Slow. Distance. . . . Also known as LSD in running. It's what you'll be doing today." Coach Martin stood in the center of a ring of stretching runners. He put his clipboard behind his back and walked the ring our feet made as we reached for our toes. "Today's run is about enduring. It's about getting your mind to a place where it can rest and let your body take over. Don't look at your watch, don't guess the mileage, and don't think. Just run. Settle into a pace that you can hold as long as I ask you to." I didn't flinch. All the better. Bent in a stretch, I exhaled into my knees and welcomed the time to not think about anything but running.

"We're going to head back into the canyon. I'll be in front of you on my bike with water if you need it."

I leaned forward again and looked out of the corner of my eye for Jillian. She was already up on her feet, kicking out her legs. I stood up casually and stretched my arms above my head. Coach Martin glanced at each of us. "And one last thing. No racing. Let it go for today or you won't last the run. Now, let's go."

Our shoes crunched over the dirt track, first in a walk and then accelerating into a slow jog. I was conscious of Jillian a foot or so behind me, but didn't alter my pace. When she caught up and I could see her in my peripheral vision, I quelled the urge to pick it up. She looked over at me and nodded, and I nodded back. We squeezed through the gate that separated the track from the land behind the campus, and headed down a dirt road that twisted far back into the green canyon. The air was hot and dry until we rounded the first curve into it. Under the shade of towering eucalyptus trees, I began to relax into the pace and let fall away all of the things that weighed me down. I pictured the trail of them behind me—the cottage my mother had lived in; the unsettled feeling my dream had left me with; the fact that everywhere I went, someone knew something about my past that I didn't—

"Slow down." Her words jolted me from my thoughts. "You don't always have to run like you're racing. Relax."

I checked my pace. "Sorry. It's been a long day."

"Well, it's gonna get even longer. He wasn't joking about

this being a distance day. So relax. Breathe." She smiled over at me. "Tell me about you and Tyler Evans."

I tried not to react, but felt a tiny wave of nervousness zing through me. "Nothing to tell, really."

She gave me a look as our shoes crunched together in rhythm. "Come on . . . spill it. We need something to talk about to take up this run."

I glanced around, cheeks burning. At our pace we'd left the rest of the girls trailing some distance behind. Her tone was easy and comfortable, so I figured it was safe. "All right. There's nothing *interesting* to tell. We were both at this life-guard bonfire, and we swam out to jump this rock, and I gave him every opening I possibly could have to make a move, but he didn't. And I wasn't naked. Or drunk." I paused and glanced over at Jillian, who was smiling knowingly. "Too bad the truth doesn't live up to the rumors, huh?"

She rolled her eyes. "It never does. I figured it was some-thing like that. Don't worry about it. People just like to talk. They'll forget by Friday." We took a few more strides before she spoke again. "And don't count Tyler out either. For all his cockiness, he's actually kind of a gentleman, so I'm not sur-prised he didn't do anything. It's probably a good sign, actually. If you're into him."

Oh, God. "Did you guys . . . I'm sorry. I had no idea—"

She laughed out loud. "*Me?* Oh, *God*, no. I didn't date Tyler. No offense, but he's not really my type." We'd picked up the pace the slightest bit. "No, my sister went out with him a few times, and she said the same thing about him. That he passed up a few good moments before he actually kissed her. "

The previous moment's awkwardness paled in comparison to this. What was I supposed to say? That I knew about her sister? Ask about her? Say I was sorry? That I'd banish Tyler from my thoughts? I was so used to being on the other side of this conversation, I had no idea. "Oh, I . . ."

"You don't have to feel weird about it, though. She's been gone for a couple of years—a bad car accident. Everyone else here knows, so you may as well hear it from me. Anyway, you should go for it. He's a good guy."

She'd done perfectly what I'd never been able to do. Slipped it in casually, like she was long over it, and got on with the conversation. She hadn't even left me room to say "I'm sorry" before moving on to Tyler. But I couldn't not acknowledge it.

"Wow. I'm so sorry. About your sister, I mean." I fumbled, but she rescued me.

"It is what it is. Sometimes life throws shitty surprises at you and there's nothing you can do about it, you know?"

I nodded and inhaled deeply. It would have been a good moment to say "Yeah, I know what you mean" or something that let her know I'd been there too. That I was back there, in a way. But I didn't. Instead I cleared my mind of everything except the rhythm of our feet in the dirt, my breaths, and the quiet understanding I felt growing between us as we matched strides.

15

Friday came more quickly than I'd expected. I'd spent the week waking up looking forward to first period, where Tyler and I snuck friendly banter back and forth when Mr. Strickland wasn't looking. My lunches were spent listening to Ashley and the two girls she'd befriended in dance class chatter about everyone in school, from who they were dating to who they were wearing. I got myself transferred to a different English class so I wouldn't have to face Joy again. And Jillian and I had just taken first and second in the opening meet, helping earn a win for our team. And now it was Friday.

We walked out to the parking lot, still in our uniforms, and she stopped when we got to her car. "Wanna go to the party at Celine's tonight? It's tradition after the first race . . ." She threw her bag into the trunk. I was about to take her up on the offer, but we both turned at the voice that came from across the lot.

"Hey! Louanna!"

Jillian raised an eyebrow. "Or maybe you have other plans?"

I tried to tone down the immediate giddiness that spread out from my stomach. "No. Not yet. . . . Maybe?" I could always hope.

"Let's leave it open, then." She got into her car. "Call me if you decide you want to come, and I'll pick you up." Before I had a chance to answer, she winked, shut the door, and was backing out.

Tyler jogged up behind me. "Hey, I was trying to call you." I could hear the grin in his voice and I paused before turning, mostly to compose myself.

"Funny. I could have sworn you heard me tell Mr. Strickland that I go by 'Anna.'"

"I heard you and Jillian killed it in your race today. Anna. Nicely done." He smiled his golden-boy smile at me, and that, in combination with his hair all wet and sticking up in every direction, was enough to make me—well, I didn't even know.

He smelled like chlorine, but I liked it on him. "Did you guys have a game today?" I grinned inwardly at a brief flash in my mind of him in a Speedo and the funny little water polo cap.

"No. First one's next week."

"Oh." For lack of a better response, I took a step toward my car.

Tyler went with me. "So, I didn't ever get to ask you—how was your dad about the whole party thing? I figure I don't have a job next summer, after that."

I kicked a rock across a few empty parking spaces. "He was pretty pissed, but I think he'll let it go. He's done a few things that he owes me an apology for, so I'm gonna say we're even."

"What, like naming you Louanna?"

I gave him a look. "That was my mom's fault, actually. It was after her grandmother or something like that."

"If it makes you feel any better, my real first name is Frank. Tyler is my middle name. But same thing. I'm named after the grandpa I never met."

I stopped at the back of my bus. "This is me."

"Yeah?" He eyed the surf racks on top of the bus.

"Yep." I opened the back window and threw my backpack in, then turned back to him and tried to think of something else to say.

"The classic surf mobile." He smiled wide. "It suits you."

I smiled back. I had always loved the bus. "Yeah, we've been a lot of places in that thing. I'm not sure that it fits in here, though." I looked across the half-empty parking lot that held a mix of BMWs, Mercedes, and Range Rovers.

He waved his hand dismissively. "Cars like that are a waste. They've never been down a dirt road in Mexico that ended at the perfect surf spot." He patted the back window. "This one, though . . . I bet it's seen some pretty cool places."

We were quiet a moment, and I looked at the ground. "I should get going," I managed, sounding as awkward as I felt. I didn't mention the party. Just in case he was about to invite me somewhere. I pinched my running jersey between my two fingers. "Gotta get out of this thing." *Lovely. Remind him how gross and stinky you are right at this moment.*

Tyler didn't seem to notice. "Yeah, I should get going too. My dad has some big business meeting late, and I promised my mom I'd go to dinner with her . . ." He trailed off, and we both stood, unmoving. I was about to break the long moment of silence, but I saw something flicker over his face and waited. "Hey. Just so you know, those cottages you were asking about—all the broken-down ones? Most of them aren't locked up. You wouldn't need your dad's keys to go look in them. You just have to find an open lock. I went through them all last summer. Kind of another rookie initiation."

I raised an eyebrow and gave him my best mischievous smile. "Oh, yeah? Well, I'll keep that in mind—although . . . I'd be too creeped out to go in them alone, and my dad is working nights now, so he couldn't take me. But, yeah, one of these days I'll have to check them out." I couldn't have left him a bigger opening. I waited. Hoped. Opened the driver's side door and started to climb in.

He took a step closer and leaned a tanned arm on the open door. "Hey—"

I caught my breath and got ready to accept his offer to give me a full tour of the cottages.

"You should ask James. He knows all about the history of them and all that stuff—if *that's* what you're really interested in." He was looking straight at me with his ridiculous silver-blue eyes and the hint of a smile.

I put the key into the ignition, turned it hard, and did my best at nonchalance, despite the heat that crept up my neck. "Yeah, that's right. James." I looked at my watch. "Maybe we'll check them out tonight. He'll probably just be getting off duty when I get home, if I go soon." I put my sunglasses on. He stepped backward, then shut the door softly for me. His hands rested on the open window frame, inches away from my shoulder.

I shrugged. "If not, maybe I *will* just bring a flashlight and go myself."

He laughed a little, then looked down at his feet.

"What?" I asked, a bit more indignant-sounding than I would have liked.

He grinned at me and put his hands up. "Nothing, nothing. . . . I could show them to you one of these days too, if *that's* what you're interested in."

I paused, trying to determine if this offer was out of sincerity, interest, amusement . . .

"Yeah? If you ever want to come down, you know where I live." I smiled and put the bus in reverse. "Otherwise, I'll see ya around," I said brightly, hoping that it sounded casual, but mortified he had read me that easily.

He pushed off the door and waved as he took a step back. "Bye, Anna."

I nodded when I drove by, and he did the same. In the rearview mirror, I watched as he kicked a rock, sending it bouncing across the asphalt. Then he shook his head and laughed, and I was sure the humorous thing was me. Ugh.

It was close to five by the time I parked the bus in front of our cottage. I shut the motor off and looked out through the windshield for a moment, straight at my mom's cottage. I didn't even know she'd lived in it. Had she grown up there? Spent summers? How many nights had she stood on the tiny balcony and breathed the ocean air?

A wave broke the stillness, and I shook the thoughts from my head before getting out. I looked up to the north end of the beach, where falling-down cottages dotted the hill and the bluff above. The sun hung low in the sky, spilling orange warmth onto them. CRYSTAL COVE BEACH COTTAGES: ISLANDS IN TIME ON THE CALIFORNIA COAST. That's what the sign over the little park store said. Again, I had a feeling maybe that's what my dad was after in coming back here. To go back to an easier, happier time in his life. I could see the draw, the charm he saw in it. His history ran deeper here than I had ever cared to ask about. My mother's, too, which was the problem. I'd done all my asking about her a long time ago, taken the simple answers, and packaged them up neatly in the back of my mind. And it would have been easy for them to stay that way had we not ended up here, on an island in time.

I pushed the thought from my head and headed up the front steps, but stopped short when something on the doormat caught my eye. It was a small folded piece of paper, weighted down with a cobalt blue piece of sea glass. With my name scrawled on the front.

I stared at it, running through the few possible people it could be from. But the sea glass narrowed it down to only one, and I felt guilty just thinking about her. After that first day of school, I never went back to Joy's class. Getting switched to another English teacher was surprisingly easy once I told my counselor what was mostly the truth—that I couldn't take Joy seriously as a teacher when she'd been such a close family friend. Since then I'd done the best I could to put her and all she knew about my mom out of my mind. I'd wanted to at least bring her book back, but each day I carried it in my backpack, I found another reason to avoid her hallway altogether.

I set my bag down and knelt to pick up the glass and the note. Then I sat on the front step, placed the still-folded note in my lap, and examined the glass in the afternoon sun. It was the size of a small marble, time-smoothed and thick, and the color blue that could have been a vase, or a medicine bottle, or . . . a mermaid tear. I stared down at the note, and waited a breath before I opened it.

Dear Anna,

Found this on the beach today and I knew you would appreciate it. I want you to know, I understand your choice to leave my class. I shouldn't have assumed you'd want to talk about your mother with me. For that, I'm sorry. I knew a sparkling, artistic side of her and would love to share that with you one day. But I realize that sometimes our histories can feel too fragile to sift through. If you decide you'd like to, come find me. And please, keep the book. It was a source of inspiration for her.

Maybe it can be for you, too.

Fondly,

Joy

I sat still, aware only of the rhythmic crash and rush of the waves and the closing-in sensation all around me. I wanted to know about her, I did. I ached to. But I worried that Joy was wrong. That it wasn't history that was too fragile, but me. I folded the note up tiny and shoved it down into my bag, along with the glass. Not tonight. Tonight I'd go out with Jillian, away from the cove, and I'd feel better.

When I emerged from the steamy bathroom, our house all golden—warm with late afternoon sunlight—it seemed like forgetting about it all might actually work.

16

Jillian wasn't answering her phone, but I wasn't in a big hurry. I had no idea what the dress code might be for the party, so I pulled on some comfy shorts and a tank top and plunked myself down in my green chair to wait for her to call back. Outside, the beach was deserted except for an elderly couple walking hand in hand along the waterline. They were both barefoot, with their pants rolled up to their calves, which struck me as unusual and especially sweet.

My mind wandered to Tyler and his easy confidence. I'd actually most like to be going somewhere with him tonight, but that hadn't panned out. Either he was completely oblivious or just not interested. Both possibilities ended with him being unattainable.

And then there he was. Literally. Walking down the beach, carrying a bag and drink tray from the Beachcomber.

I shot up, smoothed my hair, and sat back down, all in quick succession. A minute later, when his face appeared in one of the glass panes of our front door, I was sitting in my chair, casually flipping through the first book I'd grabbed. I was the picture of relaxation.

He knocked, and I gave a little jump, then squinted at the door like I didn't know who it could possibly be. When we made eye contact, I gave him a puzzled look, which was quickly replaced by a smile before I got up and walked over to the door as casually as I could. Then I opened the door and felt stupid. He was still in the same clothes I had left him in, and I was basically in my pj's.

Luckily, they were cute and little.

I noticed him notice. "Hi." His eyes moved quickly over me before he brought them back to my own.

I smiled, my confidence bolstered by this small thing. "I thought you had a dinner date . . ."

"Yeah, well. She stood me up. Conference call with her new business partner. So I had these burgers from up there." He motioned to the Beachcomber. "You hungry?" I scanned the beach for any sign of my dad's truck before answering, which must have caused a too-long pause.

"You do eat . . . right?"

"Yeah." I brought my eyes back to his. "Sorry. You just surprised me."

He shrugged. "I could probably eat them both if you're not interested. I was thinking I'd just sit all by myself down there on the sand and then take my flashlight and go check out some of the cottages all by myself too."

I rolled my eyes. "All right, enough. If you wanted to hang out with me that bad, you could have just asked. Lemme grab a blanket." He raised an eyebrow. "To sit on," I said flatly, though I was flattered by the implication, however tiny. I stepped back. "You can come in. I'll just be a minute." I grabbed my phone and sent Jill a quick text: "Guess I do have plans. ☺ See you Monday."

He scanned the beach just as I had a moment before, then stepped in and stood in front of the window. "So this is what you see every day. Must be nice."

I moved some pillows aside and opened one of the storage benches in the little alcove. "You saw it every day at work." I pulled out a multicolored quilt, faded and worn thin after many a day spread out on the sand.

"Yeah, I guess. But I wasn't relaxing in my living room. I was at work. You get to live the life every day." He turned slightly, so that he faced my mom's cottage, then nodded at it. "I think we should try to get in there. That's the only one I haven't been in."

"No!" I said, with more force than I had meant to. "I mean, I just think it'd be too easy to get caught in there," I covered. "Too many people walk up and peek in the windows. I watch them all the time. Plus, my dad drives by a couple times a night, and he'd notice a light in there, believe me. Let's walk up to the north ones."

"All right," he said as we walked out the door. "Let me just warn you, though—there's a reason they're condemned. Grab your shoes. And maybe a sweatshirt or something."

He stood aside for me, and I led the way down the stairs, which I was happy to do because the butterflies in my stomach felt like they must be obvious on my face. Now the night felt like possibility. So much so that I almost didn't glance over at her cottage as we made our way onto the cooling sand.

Neither one of us said anything as we spread the blanket out. I sat down, and Tyler did too, close enough so that I caught a hint of chlorine again. He pulled two paper-wrapped burgers and a box of fries out of the bag, then some napkins. He handed me one of the sodas from the tray, then held his cup up.

"Cheers. To making it through your first week at Coast." We each sipped from our straws, then he twisted his cup into the sand and leaned back on his elbows.

"So, what do you think so far?"

I cleared my throat and briefly imagined telling him that I had never found wild hair and the smell of swimming pools so attractive. "It's not too bad, I guess." I ran my fingers through the sand next to the blanket. "People are definitely different here from my last school."

He swallowed a mouthful of food and washed it down with a gulp of soda. "In a good way or a bad way?"

I looked out at the ocean and tried to suppress a smile. "I don't know yet. I'll tell you when I decide."

He nodded. "I don't doubt it. You don't seem to be the type to hold back much."

I cocked my head a bit, surprised at this. He had no idea how much I could hold back.

"Aw, come on." He grinned. "It was obvious you wanted me from the moment you saw me." I rolled my eyes. "It's okay. It happens all the time. That's why you walked over to the rocks, so I would have to talk to you."

I had to laugh. Partly because it was true. "*Actually*, my dad sent me down there to make sure you were doing your job and keeping people off the rocks. You didn't get a very good report, sorry to say."

He shrugged again. "Last week of summer. What can I say?" There was a long pause, and we both looked out at the water. The large fog bank that had been sitting on the horizon was now creeping closer.

Tyler nudged my shoulder. "So come on. What's one thing that's different here—in a good way?"

I thought about it. "I guess that people aren't exactly what I expected." He motioned for me to go on. "Well, look at Ashley. She seems like kind of . . ."

"Clueless?"

"No. I was gonna say 'prissy rich girl.' But she's actually really sweet and generous." Tyler nodded like he'd give me the benefit of the doubt on that one. "And Jillian—the first day I met her, all I wanted to do was beat her at running because she seemed so smug about it. But I kind of like that about her now." I paused for a sip of my soda. "And then you. Well. Jury's still out on that."

He grinned. "Fair enough. Maybe a tour of the cottages will help you decide. Eat something. Then I'll give you the grand tour. Your choice—pick a piece of history."

17

The sun melted into the mist all around us, and I shivered in the breeze that had carried it in. I wished I'd grabbed a sweater. Or that he'd just pull me in close to warm me up. We stood in front of a smattering of condemned cottages— all practically falling down, but each one unique. Behind the waist-high fence the state had put in, there was a boardwalk that now rolled and waved over sand and under the ice plant that had taken over. I wondered if the boardwalk had at one time spanned the length of the beach, but it didn't seem likely.

"Well?" Tyler faced the cottages. "Which one?"

I swept my eyes over the worn wood of each cottage and settled on one a few steps away. In front of it, half-buried, lay a small blue rowboat that looked like it had sunk into the sand.

"That one." I pointed. "It looks like a postcard."

"It is, in the general store. The Carter Cottage. It's also been painted a million times or so. Original choice." He stared straight ahead at the Carter Cottage, and though I did too, I could feel him smiling.

"Hey, you said it was my choice. That one looks the most . . ."

"Friendly?" he finished.

"Yeah. I dunno if it's the fog or what, but they all look a little creepy right now."

He turned to face me and shrugged. "We don't have to go in if you don't want. It's mainly spiderwebs and mouse crap, anyway." I scrunched my nose. "But in a few you can find stuff that the people left behind when they had to leave."

Automatically my eyes went way down the beach, to my mother's cottage. "When did they leave again?" I asked casually.

"The state gave them their first eviction notices back in the seventies, but they fought it until around fifteen years ago." He kicked at the sand in front of him with his toes. "In these ones that haven't been redone, there's still a lot of their stuff. That's what makes the cottages kind of creepy. This one's that way. Has a story, too."

I was still looking down at the beach cottage. My mother's cottage. The possibility of anything of hers still inside made me feel heavy and slow. I swallowed and forced myself to turn my eyes back to Tyler. When I did, he grinned and nudged me.

"Still in? If you get scared . . . you know, feel free to just grab on to me, and I'll fight off the cottage ghosts." He puffed up his chest in exaggerated toughness.

He meant it as a joke, but it took everything I had to offer a smile.

I stepped over a low point in the fence. "All right then. The Carter Cottage."

✳

In the dark the smell of damp wood was the first thing I noticed. That, and that the floor felt like it was gonna give. Both were unsettling.

Tyler grabbed my elbow lightly. "Watch your step. There's holes all over the place." He flicked on the flashlight. "There."

My eyes followed the beam of light as it circled the small room. He had been right about a few things. Cobwebs hung heavily from the ceiling corners and window frames, the wood floor was dotted everywhere with tiny brown pellets, and everything was still there—a sagging couch facing the ocean, a coffee table, shadowed picture frames on the walls. I didn't move.

"It's darker in here than I thought it would be," I said, looking back toward the cracked door.

"All the shutters are closed up. These things are pretty dark even in the daytime." He stepped past me, avoiding a broken floorboard. "This one is small. Living room right here, kitchen, bathroom, and one tiny bedroom. I think it must have been where the kids slept, because there's still a set of bunk beds in there. Wanna see?"

I thought of every horror movie I'd ever watched. The ones with kids in them were always the creepiest. I tried to stall. "How do you all of a sudden know so much about these places? And why'd you play dumb about them at the bonfire?"

He led me through a narrow doorway. "Rookie hazing. Remember? We have to go through all the ones on the north side. Except that when we do it, there are dumb-ass old guards hiding everywhere, jumping out at you like idiots. James actually put his foot through the floor back there last summer."

We went into the tiny bedroom, which held the bunk beds and not much else. Tyler shined the light on their red metal frame. "What was your other question?"

I rolled my eyes in the dark. "Why you played dumb at the bonfire," I answered with feigned annoyance. Despite the overtly creepy atmosphere, I was starting to enjoy myself.

"Oh, *that*. If I'd told you all about it then, you wouldn't have gotten curious and tried to rope me into a guided tour." He put the flashlight under his chin and widened his eyes. "Guess it worked. I'm good."

"And modest." I rolled my eyes again, this time sure that there was enough light for him to see me. Then I looked around the room, which was mostly empty, aside from the beds. In the corner was a tiny wooden picnic table. I pointed to it. "Shine the light over there for a second." He did, and I stepped over another hole in the floor, then stood over the table.

Tyler came up behind me and curved his arm around me to put the flashlight directly over the table. It took everything in me not to lean back into him.

"I wasn't gonna show you this, cuz I thought it might freak you out. It's actually the best thing I've found in all the cottages. Kind of the saddest, too, though."

I stared at the tabletop below me. Underneath a clear layer, probably surfboard resin, black-and-white images of two kids, a boy and a girl, smiled up at us. The entire surface of the table was a collage of the two light-haired kids at different ages, all over the beach. In one I recognized the cottage in the background. The kids sat on the boardwalk in front of it, hanging their tan legs over the edge. In another they stood proudly in front of a little boat, with their dad, I assumed. He had the same light eyes and crinkly smile. I ran my hand over the smooth surface.

"I can't believe they didn't take this when they left. It's like their whole childhood down here."

"I know," Tyler said.

I leaned down and looked at another image of the kids, who stood silhouetted side by side, looking out the living room window at the ocean. "They must have hated leaving here."

Tyler kept the light over the table. "Well, according to James, they didn't really leave."

"What do you mean," I asked tentatively.

"I thought he was just messing with us when he told it, but he swears up and down that those two kids and their mom drowned under that little blue boat out there."

Chills went through me, and I stared at the picture of them in front of the boat. "*Under* it?" Something about this sounded vaguely familiar.

"Yeah. In, like, three feet of water. On a sunny day with small surf." My stomach went queasy. I knew this story. I'd heard my dad tell it to rookie guards during training, to keep them from being complacent. I'd had no idea it had happened here. Tyler went on. "The dad took them out, just to go paddle around. It was a calm day, but a big set wave came and flipped the boat." I bit my lip, knowing what was coming, unable to take my eyes away from the smiling faces of the kids and their father. "The dad got thrown from the boat first." Tyler paused and looked down at the pictures.

I nodded, the scenario playing out in my head, now with faces to put to it. I knew from my dad's story that the father had been thrown from the boat, and that while he'd struggled in the shore break, a second wave had pounded his wife and kids, and that, unfortunately, they'd clung to each other and the boat before it had flipped over. I could hear my dad's voice as he told the story of the family trapped beneath their little boat in three feet of water. A freak accident on a placid day.

I interrupted Tyler. "That was one of my dad's first rescues. He was the first one to get to the boat, then the dad was there too, and he said they could hear the kids and the mom yelling from under it." When my dad told the story to the rookie classes, he spoke about how the boat had landed in a depth of water, at such an angle, that it was literally suctioned to the sand. He told them about how the strength of all the people on the beach who rushed into the water to help wasn't enough to loose it from the sand. How eventually, they'd had to wait for the tide to come up, and the inevitable. And he told them how they could never take the ocean for granted and how he would always be reminded of that fact by the memory of muffled voices from beneath that boat, on a sunny day, in water that barely covered his knees. There weren't many things that could stun a group of cocky new guys into silence, but my dad's voice when he told that story was one of them.

That same silence fell over Tyler and me now, and I searched for a way to break it. "So the dad just left after that? Left everything here?"

Tyler swept the flashlight around the room. "Yeah. I would have too. There's no way I could stay and look out at the place where my whole family died right in front of me."

My chest squeezed hard, forcing the air out of me slowly. I had. For nine years. I'd stared straight out at cold, black water, apologizing for whatever it was I'd done and willing her to come back, wondering what I could have done differently.

Tyler turned to me. "You okay? You wanna get outta here?"

"Yeah. I . . . I need some fresh air, I think." He looked at me for a long moment, trying to decipher what had changed. I swallowed the lump in my throat and tried to sound normal. "Let's go." I ushered him in front of me and tentatively put my hand on his shoulder as we made our way back out to the door.

It was lighter than I expected it to be when we stepped onto the porch of the Carter Cottage. The tang of the salt air, coupled with the smack of a wave, opened my chest up and I breathed in deeply. Tyler was looking at me, his flashlight pointed at our feet. I raised my eyes to meet his and hoped that he couldn't see what I had felt.

"You get a little spooked in there?"

"Yeah. Sorry. That was . . ."

"It's okay. I don't blame you." We were quiet a moment, and he smiled. "Although I did *warn* you it was creepy." A stray strand of my hair rose with the breeze, and I shivered, then tucked it away behind my ear.

"You cold?" Tyler unzipped his hoodie and took a step closer, offering it. It was, of course, a nice gesture. In a different moment I might have thought of it as cliché, maybe even laughed it off or teased him a little. Now, though, it felt like a prelude to a moment of possibility, and the thought made me tingly with anticipation.

"Thanks." Smiling, I slid my arms into the too-big sleeves that were still warm, and pulled it tight around me.

"Wanna walk a little?"

I nodded, and we stepped off the porch and back over the fence onto the sand. The fog had risen to form a hazy white ceiling above us, and the few nearby lights reflected off it, creating a pale glow. We walked in the wet sand at a slow, meandering pace with no destination other than, in my mind, the moment we had missed out on more than once before. I glanced over at Tyler, who picked up a pebble and rubbed the sand from its surface with his thumb. He stopped abruptly, then raised his eyes to mine and opened his mouth like he was going to say something. I waited. Breathlessly would be only a slight exaggeration. Then he turned and chucked the pebble into the water, where it skipped over the surface twice before disappearing. "So is your curiosity satisfied now?" Tyler asked, taking a step to keep going.

I wanted to be bold. Tell him no, it wasn't. Stop him, turn, and lean in close—so close, he couldn't mistake it for anything else.

"Maybe," I managed. "I might want to see some of the other ones, though, another time." Not quite as bold as I'd imagined, but it still left an opening. We walked side by side.

A smile, not a smirk, spread over his face, and he looked over at me, our footsteps slowing. "I think that could be arranged." In the pale light reflected off the water and the clouds, I could just make out his eyes, looking at me intently, and I knew we were close. All it would take was a step forward, a tilt of the head, a tiny risk. The seconds stretched out between us.

I stopped walking and turned to face him. "Good. Because I . . . You . . ."

I saw his head tilt slightly as he leaned in, and before I had time to think about it, his hand was warm on my cheek. And he kissed me. A slow, sweet kiss that was confident and gentle at the same time, that tasted like salt, and mint gum, and perfection, and that seemed to ask a question he already knew the answer to. I melted into it entirely, and in that moment nothing else existed. We lingered there after, our foreheads tilted together, not sure what to say.

Then Tyler whipped his head back abruptly.

"Shit." He was looking past me, down the beach. "Headlights."

I spun around. "That's my dad." We watched the beams rise and fall over the sand at the south end of the beach, definitely coming our direction. "He's going to my house. Dinner."

Tyler was taking off his shoes. "Run. You need to run home. Now. Go."

I burst out laughing and slid my sandals off. "Are you *serious*?"

"Yeah, I'm serious. What do you think he's gonna do if he gets home and you're not there? Go." He was laughing too, shaking his head. "Shit."

"Okay, okay." I took a step, then turned around. "Where are you going?"

"Home. I'll see you tomorrow." He stood barefoot in the sand, holding his shoes and the flashlight.

I didn't move.

He pointed at the light beams still making their way up the beach. "Go, or he's gonna have Newport Beach PD out here looking for you."

"All right." I smiled. "I'm going."

I turned, then glanced back to see Tyler, in the lights of the dirt road, making his way slowly onto the beach behind me, to where he would take the road up to his car. I looked around. It took a few seconds for my eyes to adjust, but once they did, I found the water's edge and broke into a run.

I couldn't remember ever having run at night. It was a different sensation altogether. I wasn't conscious of my breathing or steps at all. Just the sounds of the night as I passed them by—a wave crashing, the voices and clinking of silverware that drifted down from the restaurant, and the literal symphony of frogs in the creek bed I had heard the night we'd arrived.

I kept my eyes on the headlights as they rounded a point and then disappeared into the cove south of our house, right as I reached the bottom of our steps. I took two at a time, then all in one motion I burst through the door, flipped on the light, and threw myself into the green chair, swooping up my book on the way down. Light splashed onto the sand in front of our house, followed by the low hum of my dad's engine working its way over the dips and hills. He slowed the truck and flashed his spotlight up at the living room window. I sat up in the chair and waved enthusiastically, and he cruised right on by, continuing his patrol of the beach.

I exhaled loudly, leaned my head back on the chair, and replayed the kiss, over and over, until my breathing returned to normal. Tyler was interested. And an amazing kisser. Definitely worth missing the party for. Smiling, I snuggled down into his sweatshirt and rolled my head over to the side so I could look out the window. But I stopped abruptly when I found myself staring straight at my mom's cottage. The windows were dark, but not boarded up like the ones in the Carter Cottage. In one spot the fence leaned enough so that a person could just step right over it and find their way to the door, which was probably unlocked. I sat for a moment, wondering what it would be like to step inside it, just to see if there was anything left of her there.

I shivered and sat up, flipped to the first page of the book in my lap, and felt in my chest that same heavy sinking feeling when I read the opening sentences.

All sea goddesses inherit the sea's qualities. Just as the sea can be gentle and nurturing, or violent and deadly, so can they. They are at once beautiful and cruel, tender and selfish, vulnerable, yet unattainable. Above all, they offer shimmering glimpses into the deep ocean of secrets that is a woman's heart.

My mother had always been a mystery to me, even when she was alive. She'd been all those things, all at once, and we'd tiptoed around her even then. And now, here, she'd stirred up the placid surface of my life and thrown me into rough, dark water—a deep ocean of secrets.

I couldn't tell anyone I was flailing.

18

"Wake up, sunshine. We're goin' surfin'. Your board's in the bus, coffee's made, and we leave in five minutes." I pulled my covers up over my head.

"I'm not taking no for an answer. It's good out there."

"Where are we going?" I mumbled.

"South parking lot. Ab Rock. You know the place, I'm pretty sure." I could hear the smiling sarcasm in my dad's voice. Apparently enough time had passed that we could now joke about my misadventures. I waited for his feet to pad away down the hall, and replayed kissing Tyler for the millionth time before I got out of bed. I hadn't dreamed it. It had really happened.

A few minutes later I was pouring enough cream into my coffee to make it the same color as the sand outside. I didn't much like to drink it, but I did like the feel of the warm cup in my hand as we drove down the highway and then stood on the cliff, checking the surf. Nobody else was out yet, and the sun sparkled on the water, inviting us to be the first ones. My dad put his hand on the back of my neck and squeezed. "Seems like I haven't seen you all week. It'll be nice to get out there together. We can go get a big breakfast after."

I smiled over at him. "Sounds good." It did, but I was wary. We were going to have to talk about things at some point, and I could tell it was gonna be today, out in the water.

He took a slow sip of his coffee and watched as a set lined up. Aside from the waves, it was so quiet I wondered if he was thinking the same thing. He swallowed and nodded decisively. "All right. Let's go."

My board hit the water with a slap. I jumped on, letting it glide for a long moment before I dug my arms in to paddle. My dad was out in front of me and I concentrated on trying to keep up with the powerful strokes he always made look easy. No matter how much time had passed since he had last surfed, his strokes were sure, fast, and smooth. And no matter how in shape I thought I was, I always had to push to keep up with him. By the time I caught up, he was already straddling his board as it bobbed gently in the glassy morning water. Arms burning, I pushed myself up, and we sat, just the two of us, in the shadow of Ab Rock.

"Great morning to be out here, huh?" he said happily. "Did you see that last little set that came through?"

I nodded, and he motioned for me to paddle closer to him. "If you wanna get any of 'em, you gotta be right over here, almost on top of the rock."

I slid back onto my stomach and paddled over, eyeing the base of the rock we had both jumped off. We sat for another moment, with only the gurgling sounds of the water between us. It was peaceful, but I knew the weight of our "talk" hung over us. I also knew that my dad probably didn't know how to start, so I figured I'd just throw it out there.

"So. This is it. The place where you and Mom met." I watched him carefully for a reaction as I spoke. "Something about you being sloshed . . . jumping naked . . . off a rock . . ." I gestured up at the sheer rock cliff above us and smiled, trying to keep the tone light for as long as I could. "We never did get to talk about when *you* did it. You know, with you yelling at me and all."

He gave me a stern look that lasted only a second before it turned into a slow smile. "No, I guess we didn't. There are a *few* things we didn't get to talk about, on account of *you* yelling at *me*, too." I looked down at the bumpy white wax on my board but didn't say anything.

A swell passed under us, providing a moment, and questions bounced off each other in my mind. I decided to start small, and looked up into my dad's face. "So did you really meet her that night? When you kissed her?"

He grinned the grin that made him look young and happy. "Yeah. I spent all summer watching her on the beach, working up the nerve, and when she showed up at the party, I knew it was my last shot, because she'd be leaving soon." He smiled down at the water, remembering. "I half-expected to get slapped, but she was a good sport about it. She didn't have a choice but to fall for me after that. From that night on, if she was here, we were together."

"Hm." I watched my foot swirl around under the water, and I enjoyed the thought that they had once been young, and reckless, and happy. It was encouraging, even though I knew how the story ended.

"So she didn't live here? She just visited?"

He nodded. "The cottage belonged to her grandma, Louanna, who you're named after. *She* lived here permanently. Your mom and her parents lived up near San Francisco. They came down summers, but rented a house on Balboa Island. Only your mom stayed here, at the cottage. Louanna always had a room made up for her." His tone hardened slightly. "Her folks didn't care for it down here, though. It was too . . ." A pause. "It wasn't good enough for them." He shook his head, and in the tightening of his jaw, I started to understand. "But your mom loved it. She loved it like she'd lived here all her life. So she stayed here with her grandma. Every summer, every vacation she could."

I'd never met her parents. Had never even heard them mentioned. Growing up, my dad's mom had been my only grandparent. She lived a few blocks over from where we'd lived in Pismo Beach, and she was as much a part of my life as my parents. I never questioned it, before or after my mom was gone. Now, though, a reason took shape. Another wave passed under us, and I waited a beat before asking.

"So . . . did they not like *you*, either? Is that why I don't know them?"

He blinked, maybe taken aback at my questions, maybe at what the answers were. Then he cleared his throat and looked out over the water, and resignation settled on his face.

"No. They didn't like me. And they hated that she did. And, yes, that's why you don't know them. When she chose me, they chose not to be a part of her life." His voice was a mix I knew, sad and angry. "Or yours."

I took a deep breath, trying to understand. It didn't make sense. "Because they didn't approve of you? Because of *money* or something? That's *insane*. She was their only daughter. How does a parent even *do* that?" I was surprised at how indignant I felt, but it sounded like the most ridiculous, old-fashioned thing I'd ever heard, to disown your child because she fell for someone you didn't approve of. My dad watched me without saying anything, and then I knew.

There had to be more.

More than one wave passed under us this time, but we didn't move or say anything. After what seemed like forever, he got to the more.

"We were seventeen, Anna. We had a year of school left, and then she was supposed to go off to some big college, far away, and live up to their expectations. She'd already made up her mind that she wasn't going. . . ." He paused, like he was deciding what to say. Then he cleared his throat. "When she told me about you, I was on my knees in the sand before she could finish, with a piece of sea grass for a ring, and it was the most right thing I'd ever done in my life."

He looked at me now with eyes I'd seen before. Eyes that had lost her. And I couldn't stand to look back, so I put my head down and ran my finger down the center of my surfboard. They were a year older than me. And parents.

"I'm sorry I didn't tell you sooner. You were a little girl when she died, and right after it happened, you wanted to know everything about her, like you were collecting details to remember her by. You slept with her clothes, wore her perfume, asked me to tell you the stories she used to tell." He shook his head. "You'd sit out there on the beach with me, talking about how she'd come back as a mermaid and you'd swim together in the waves. It broke my heart, but it was good to talk about her with you." He paused and looked down again before bringing his eyes back to me. "Then somewhere along the line you stopped asking, like she was just gone. And we stopped talking. . . . So I didn't tell you when we came here. I didn't know how to even start."

I felt weary. Like I was sinking. For a long time I'd put it on him that we didn't talk about her. But it had been me, too. Because the older I got, and the more I remembered, the heavier it weighed on me. It was easier to think of both her and her death as a dream, or to push it back to a place where the details were hazy and unclear, and I was never there.

I stared hard now at the beach, zipping my moonglass back and forth along its chain, wishing I had just left it alone, because now there was more, and it started with a choice she'd made before I was even born. She'd chosen my dad, and she'd chosen me. She'd left her family, and her life, and the place she'd loved behind, because of the choice she'd been forced to make. By me.

I blinked back tears and bit the inside of my cheek. My dad treaded water over to me and put his hand on my leg. "I wasn't sure about coming here at first, because of all this. But the happiest memories I have of your mother are here, and lots of people around knew her, and so I thought, now that you're older, if you started to wonder, it might be a place you could find out who she was and see her in a different light. She was really happy here."

He looked hopeful, like he wanted me to ask him more about her. He had no idea he'd just confirmed what I'd always thought, that I was a part of her unhappiness. We'd never said the word for what her death really was, but people who are happy with their lives don't just walk out into the water. He had to know that. I'd known it, somewhere deep, that things were bad, but I didn't know when it had happened. And now I realized it had begun with me.

I nodded and wiped at my tears, smoothing the surface back over, because, really, that was what we both wanted. "I'm glad you told me. And I'm so, so sorry. For . . . for how I've been, and . . . everything."

"Don't be, Anna. It's all right." Another little roller passed under us, and he motioned to the wave that was rising behind it. "Let's get this one in and go get some breakfast." I was more than ready to be finished talking about it as we slid to our bellies and paddled. The wave came beneath me, lifting me up, and I gave one more hard pull before popping to my feet, just as my dad did the same. Together we cut a wide path down the glass face of the wave, over tiny brown fish that darted across the sandy bottom, and I did my best to leave it all out in the water, a deep ocean of secrets.

19

My dad slid the door of the bus closed. "Poke-N-Eat tomorrow. Andy's coming over. If you want to invite any of your friends, that'd be fine."

I tried to picture Ashley's reaction to seeing the tail being pulled off a lobster in the backyard. Jillian was out of town for the weekend. "I think I'll pass. I don't really know anybody who'd want to get in the water."

We got in and he turned the key. "What about Tyler?" I tried not to flinch. He'd said it casually, like he had never embarrassed me in front of him, or told me to stay away, or anything. He had to know. He had to have seen us, or something.

I shrugged. "I'm not really friends with him. I just met him on the beach, that's all." Flimsy.

He put his hands up. "I'm just saying . . . if you want to invite him down, that's fine with me. He seems like a pretty good kid. James says he is. And it's better than having the two of you sneak around together. I do know that."

I watched him out of the corner of my eye as we backed up, debating about how to respond without getting myself into trouble. "Okay. Maybe. Thanks, Dad." He smiled wryly as we pulled onto the highway and headed south for Laguna. I rolled my window down, let the cool air rush over me, and cleared my mind of everything but Tyler.

I'd been afraid Tyler might say no. Not only because there was this whole business about my dad being his boss, but because we hadn't talked since our kiss, and he hadn't called back when I'd left a message inviting him over. But when I came up from the beach in the late afternoon on Sunday, he was sitting at the picnic table on our back patio, talking with my dad about lifeguarding like they were old friends. It was a little unnerving. I ran a hand through my hair and then walked over to the hose to rinse my feet.

"You made it." I smiled, turning the faucet.

"Of course I made it. It's my first invitation to the traditional Sunday Poke-N-Eat. I've heard about it since my first year here." He smirked at me, and I shook my head and rubbed the last of the sand off the tops of my toes, a little irritated he hadn't told me he was coming. I wasn't sure how to navigate with my dad around. Andy walked up the steps carrying his dive gear and a six-pack just in time to save me from having to come up with something.

"Anna Banana!" He set his stuff down on the table, used the edge of it to open two beers, and handed one to my dad. When he saw Tyler, his face went serious, which struck me as comical. Andy had always been protective, but when it came to me having anything to do with guys, he felt it was his duty to inform and protect me from the ones he thought were most like himself. When I turned thirteen, he pulled me aside and we had his version of "the talk," which mostly consisted of a bunch of "uhs" and "ums," but I got the gist of his speech: boys only wanted one thing, and I shouldn't give it to them until I was at least thirty-three. And married.

Before I had a chance to make any introductions, Tyler stood up and walked over to him, hand extended. "How's it goin'? I'm Tyler."

Andy took another drink and stood up tall, looking Tyler over before shaking his hand. "Andy. You must be a friend of Anna's?"

Tyler nodded easily. "Yeah, we go to school together."

"He guards down here too," I added. "He came for the Poke-N-Eat." I looked around for something I could use to distract Andy from any questions or lectures.

"No friend for you this time? What happened to Tamra?" I pictured her staring, teary-eyed, out the window at the shack, and I felt a little guilty for how I had acted at the last Poke-N-Eat. "I didn't scare her off, did I?"

"Tamra? Nah, you didn't scare her. She was too high mainte-nance." Tyler looked at me quizzically, which I brushed off, and Andy took another gulp of his beer, then exhaled loudly. "I've been thinkin' I should spend some time on my own anyway." He looked over at my dad, who was sitting in one of the chairs, the amuse-ment clear on his face. "We going out north or south tonight?"

My dad set down his beer and leaned back in the chair, stretching both arms above his head, surveying the water. "I don't know yet. Wanna go take a look?"

I glanced over at Tyler, who was pointedly looking out at the beach.

Andy finished off his beer and stifled a burp. "Yeah, sure."

"We won't be long," my dad said, eyeing me. "Go ahead and get your gear out. We're going scuba tonight."

I nodded and tried to suppress a smile as they tromped down the stairs. Tyler walked over to the tub that held his dive gear and started pulling out his weights, fins, and mask. I leaned on the picnic table, watching him and feeling the last of the afternoon sun sink into my skin. Once my dad and Andy were down on the sand, he looked up at me with a wide smile that made me sure of myself with him.

"I can't believe how hot it is down here still." He pulled his shirt up over his head, then came over and leaned on the table next to me. He was right. The air hung perfectly still and heavy around us. Even the ocean looked lazy, virtually flat with only the occasional ripple splashing up onto the sand.

"Ah, you just wanted an excuse to take your shirt off in front of me."

He raised his eyebrows and looked me over. "Says the girl who only ever wears a bikini."

I laughed nervously, then looked at my toenails that needed to be painted, the water, my bathing suit top, anything but him, because I was suddenly aware of how close we were standing.

"So now that my dad's not your boss, he's not scary anymore, huh?"

He shrugged. "James says he's not so bad. That he actually is a pretty good guy." I bit my lip to keep from smiling, and reminded myself to thank James later on.

He noticed and turned to face me. "What?"

"Nothing." I shook my head. "I'm just wondering if James

actually runs the beach. He seems to know everything."

Tyler shrugged his brown shoulders again. "Well, he's been around awhile." The smirk appeared again at the corners of his mouth, stretching out the seconds before he spoke again.

"I also had to see if you were actually going to get in the water and dive instead of just working on your tan, cuz that would be impressive."

I gave him an exasperated look. Then I kept looking for longer than I meant to. He didn't look away either, and I thought how easy it would be to just lean in and kiss him. So much easier after the first one.

The moment dissolved when Andy's and my dad's voices drifted up from the beach. I turned from Tyler and walked over to the wall where my wet suit lay draped, then bent slowly, pointedly, to pick up my fins from the ground.

"Yes," I said, smiling. "I will be diving. And I'd be willing to bet that you'll be impressed."

After a good amount of jumping around, yanking at wet suits, and weighting ourselves down, we trudged out onto the dusky beach, bent forward under our air tanks. The water lapped gently at the beach, almost like a lake, and the moon spread a glittering path out toward the rocks. It was more serene and beautiful than the night we'd arrived. We all stood at the waterline taking it in for a moment, then Tyler looked over at me and pulled the hood of his wet suit over his head.

"I can't believe you get to look out your window and see this every night." He pulled his gloves on.

"It's pretty amazing."

I hoped my voice didn't give away the ripples of apprehension that were now spreading out from the pit in my stomach. My dad stepped over to Tyler and me and gave the same instructions he did every time we went out.

"Try to keep us in sight. If you get turned around or lose us, look for no longer than a minute, then surface. We'll do the same thing. If anything happens, remember to let all your air out from your vest and kick up slower than your bubbles."

A flash of our last dive came and went, and I wondered what I would do if I thought I caught a glimpse of her again. I shook off the ridiculousness of the thought and watched as Andy and my dad switched on their lights. My dad turned to Tyler and me.

"Got your lights?"

"Yep," we answered.

"Check your pressure . . . compass . . . mask?"

"Yeah, Dad," I answered curtly. The longer we stood there looking at the water, the more anxious I felt. I tried to tell myself it was because Tyler was there, or that it was my first night dive in a long time, but it wasn't the excited anticipation kind of nervous. It was pit-in-your-stomach disquiet.

My dad ignored my tone and motioned at my fins. "You check your straps after the last dive? They were looking a little worn."

"Dad, I got it," I said impatiently. "I'll be fine. Besides"—I tried to sound nicer—"I'm with three lifeguards."

"All right. Once we're out there, keep your eyes on the crevices and rocks. The lobsters will be hanging out there. Tyler, you gone out for lobsters before?"

"No, sir, but I can't wait to bring a few home."

"Well, the easiest way to do it is to pin 'em down." He demonstrated with a quick hand motion. "Then, once you have a good hold, measure 'em and get 'em into your bag. They'll fight you, though, so be ready."

Tyler nodded, and I could tell he was looking forward to it.

"Okay. Let's go." My dad pulled his mask down over his face, flicked on his light, and walked out into the water, stopping chest-deep to put his fins on. I watched as the light went under with him and became the center of an illuminated green patch of water that slowly moved away from the shore.

Tyler spit into his mask and rubbed it around with his thumbs. "So you really go out there and grab at those things, huh?"

I scoffed. "Uh . . . no. They scare the crap out of me. Truly. They're like giant bugs. I just like to go along for the dive." I pulled on my gloves, then stretched my mask over my forehead. "But I do eat them. Tacos are the best way. I bought all the stuff for them today, so hopefully you guys will come through." I forced a smile, then stuck my regulator into my mouth and tested it out.

"All right, then," he said, and smiled. "Tacos it is."

I popped my ears all the way down to the bottom, then looked at my depth gauge. Thirty-six feet. Our lights cut bright beams through the water and illuminated the tiny particles that hung suspended in liquid green. Tyler checked his compass and pointed in the direction of the rocks. I nodded, motioning for him to lead. He pushed off with the tip of his fin, and we cruised along the bottom, which was barren and sandy. Up ahead I could see the beginning of the rocks, silhouetted in the moonlight.

I kicked easily next to Tyler as we hovered over the sand. He looked at me through his mask and nodded, which I returned, and I enjoyed not having to think of something to say. When quiet moments fell over us above the water, it was awkward, and I almost always made a wiseass remark to cover that. But down here I didn't have to.

We reached the edge of the rocks just as a stream of bubbles danced up from behind them, and my dad came into view holding a good-size lobster in the beam of his light. He stuffed it into his net bag and gave us an okay sign, checking to make sure that we were all right. We answered by returning the sign. He nodded and then pointed down at the rocks and swept his hands wide, indicating that this was the area to be looking around in. Tyler shined his light below us into a crevice and illuminated several lobsters, all waving their antennae and backing up at the same time.

Not interested in trying for them, I surveyed the rocky area around us. Some distance away, buried in the rocks, I could see the faint glow of another light. An image from the dream I'd had flashed in my mind: my mom, searching endlessly for something she'd lost. For a split second my stomach lurched, before logic told me it was Andy. Even so, my breaths came a little quicker and I had to make an effort to slow down and keep them even. Night dives were always a little eerie for me, but the last one had been unsettling.

Tyler was just ahead of me, pulling himself along the bottom edge of the rocky reef, with my dad in front of him a little ways. While they were absorbed in searching out lobsters, I hung back a bit and tried to occupy my mind with Tyler, and running, and school. Whatever might hold off images of my mom. But the images twisted and swirled around me in the water, rising like the smoke of a just-extinguished candle.

Up ahead Tyler's light went still, and I saw him make a grab. The lobster escaped and shot around him, doing zigzags before disappearing into the dark water beyond us. My dad turned to him and flashed him the okay sign again, and Tyler gave it back. When I caught up to them and they both checked with me too, I put my gloved index finger to my thumb, answering that I was okay. It was easy to lie underwater. A lot easier than having to control my voice or avoid eye contact. Or put it all out of my mind. I'd been so good at it for so long, but now something was rising slowly, making its way up through cold, black, winter water, and no matter how hard I pushed, it wouldn't go back down.

I was definitely not okay.

The air flowed easily in and out of my regulator, at a steady rhythm, but I couldn't breathe. I needed to get out.

I saw my chance as I followed the deep crevice until it widened and I could see it was lined with spiky purple urchins. Calmly and deliberately I used my right heel to push the fin strap off my left one. I felt it release, and I watched as the fin descended in slow motion into the crack, before coming to rest on a bed of urchins. Then I kicked hard to catch up and grabbed my dad's ankle, shaking it to get his attention. He turned around slowly, and I pointed to my foot, which now only wore a neoprene bootie. Then I pointed down into the crevice. Through his mask I could see he was pissed. He flashed his light to get Tyler's attention, and when Tyler swam over, my dad gave the signal for us to surface. We let all the air out of our vests and then began the kick upward, where the light of the moon waved above us, and I started to relax a little in spite of the fact that my dad was not going to be happy. When our heads broke the surface, I was waiting for it.

"Dammit, Anna," he spit out, along with his regulator. "I *asked* you about your fins." He pulled his mask up to his forehead, then shook his head. "I guess you're done for the night." Tyler didn't say anything, but looked from one of us to the other.

"I'm sorry." And I genuinely was. I had just lost a perfectly good fin on purpose, but it was better than having to explain why I didn't want to be out there. "You guys stay out. I'll kick in and start getting dinner stuff ready. You already got a couple, right?"

He brightened a little at this and looked down at his bag. "Yeah, it's good out here. Which is why you should have checked your fins." He looked over my shoulder to the lights of our house. "That's a long kick in. I don't want you doing it by yourself with one fin." He sighed, then looked at Tyler, and I could almost hear him weighing his options. Tyler must have too.

"I can go in with her," he offered. He said it almost grudgingly, but I had a feeling it was meant to sound that way.

I played too. "I'll be fine, you guys. It's not that far." I looked at both of them, and my dad shook his head.

"No, not by yourself." He turned to Tyler. "If you're volunteering, I'll stay out here and have my limit in half an hour."

Tyler nodded. "Sure. No problem. I got to grab at a few, at least."

"I would say you could come back out and find us," my dad offered, "but by the time you did, we'd probably be done. And I don't want you getting lost out here either." He sighed and shook his head yet again. "You two go on in. We shouldn't be too long. And, Anna, be sure you rinse your gear." He pulled down his mask and pushed on it until it suctioned to his face.

Then he stuck his regulator into his mouth and gave a little wave before going back under. That had worked out better than I'd thought it would.

Tyler and I were left bobbing on the slick surface only a few feet out of the bright path of moonlight. He inflated his vest and floated on his back, face to the sky. "I guess Andy's not the only one with high-maintenance girl problems. Lose a fin, require a private escort in. . . . Must be rough to be you."

"Shut up." I splashed at him. "That's not high maintenance. That's faulty equipment. And I would have made it in fine. He's just like that because . . . of his job. He has to be." I kicked my single fin so that I floated on my back next to him. He didn't say anything, and we both drifted there, looking up at the moon. Just as the quiet started to feel awkward, I pictured how ridiculous we must look, covered in neoprene from head to toe, floating on our backs with our vests fully inflated, and I couldn't help but laugh.

"What?" Tyler strained to lift his head out of the water.

"Nothing. I'd like to see a picture of this is all."

He grinned, then stuck his fins up out of the water. "You want one for the swim in?"

"I think I can manage. I don't want to be too high maintenance or anything." I lay back and started my uneven kick.

"Suit yourself." He put his head back into the water and started to kick too, passing me almost immediately.

By the time I dragged myself onto the sand, my legs were worthless. I had cursed myself the entire way for not taking him up on his fin offer. Pride had forced me to finish, but I didn't even care about that anymore. I flopped down on the wet sand and leaned back on my tank to catch my breath while Tyler stood looking out at the water.

He pointed. "I can see their lights."

"You can go back out there if you want to," I said, panting. "I'm all safe now."

He turned and looked to our lighted windows. "You gonna make it across the sand and up those stairs? You sound like you might die or something." He smiled. "You're a runner. I'd think you'd be in better shape than that."

I lay back completely on my tank and looked up at the sky. "When I run, I get to wear shoes on both feet." I closed my eyes and listened to the ripples of water on sand. "I'm comfortable right here."

"Yeah . . . I get that, but let's get out of this gear and then come back down or something. This stuff's just a little bit heavy to be standing out here enjoying the night."

"Okay." I took a deep breath and rolled onto my side so that I could push myself off the sand. Tyler grabbed my elbow and helped me up, which made me smile even as I lost my balance and tipped back over.

"Come on. Put a little effort into it." He hoisted me up again with a grunt, but I was a lost cause. After several more attempts I finally got to my feet, and we plodded up to the patio, where we went our separate ways—me to the warmth of the shower to rinse off the salt water and wet suit smell, and him to the outdoor shower my dad had rigged up.

I stepped back out onto the cool stones of the patio as he was rubbing his hair dry with a towel, still shirtless. It was hard not to stare, so I walked out to where I could see the water and felt a tiny zing of possibility when I saw two lights still circling below the surface far, far down the beach.

Tyler came over and stood next to me. "Damn. Look how light it is out there. We probably didn't even need our lights." The tide was far out, and in the moonlight I could see the slick surface of the wet sand, dotted with dark spots that were probably small rocks. I wondered if there were any pieces of glass scattered among them. Another wave of uneasiness swelled in my stomach before I willed it down and looked back over at Tyler.

He smiled. "Wanna go for a walk?"

20

I dug my toes into the wet sand and soaked up the dreamy barefoot feeling of the beach at night. In the dark the effect of everything was heightened—the moonlight, the warm air, softly lapping water . . . all of it. We walked the waterline, tiny ripples occasionally spilling over our feet, our hands brushing accidentally, suspended between nervousness and anticipation.

I snuck a glance at Tyler. He smiled, and I knew he'd felt me looking. Instead of saying anything, though, he stopped abruptly and picked something up, rubbing the sand from its surface with his thumb before holding it out to me. "It's sea glass, right?" I took it and felt the familiar smoothness between my fingers before I held it up in the moonlight, exposing its translucent green edges.

"It's—" My throat caught a little as I said the word. "It's moonglass."

"What?"

I shook my head and smiled. "I made it up when I was little. It's sea glass. But my mom and I used to go look for it whenever there was a full moon, and the pieces we found at night I called moonglass."

I could distinctly feel the slight weight of my pendant where it rested on my chest. "Like this," I said, holding it out, away from my neck. "I found this one at night." Tyler leaned in and peered at the glass triangle that dangled from my chain, and I kept talking. "It's hard to tell right now, but it's red. Which is really hard to find. Probably the most rare." *Stop talking. He's right there, so close.* Our faces were inches away from each other, looking together at the piece of red glass that spun on its chain.

Tyler seemed intrigued. "I wondered about that necklace. You always wear it."

I looked down at the glass, then let it fall back to my chest. "I was proud of this one, because it was actually me that found it, not my mom." I paused, surprised by what I was saying, but then went on, unable to stop. "She actually didn't even know I was on the beach when I found it."

"What, you snuck out or something?"

"Sort of." We resumed our walking. "I kind of followed her out one night, without her knowing." I kept talking, even as I wondered what I was doing. "I used to lie in bed and listen to her move around the house before I fell asleep, you know? Wash dishes and all that. My dad worked nights back then too, so it was always just us." It sounded almost nostalgic, put that way. "Anyway. I was listening, and I heard the front door open and close, and then it was quiet. I peeked out my window and saw her walking down the path to the beach, and it was a full moon, so I knew she'd be looking for glass. That was like our special thing." I looked down at the sand for a moment. "I got really mad that she hadn't taken me, so I ran out after her."

I was conscious of omitting details as I spoke. How we hadn't taken any walks together for a long time because she'd insisted on being alone. How I had wished every night that my dad didn't have to go to work and leave us alone together, because I never knew what kind of night it would be.

Some nights we cuddled together on the porch watching the sunset, then she would sit me up on the kitchen counter and tell me stories of mermaids while she hummed and flitted around the kitchen making dinner. I drank in her warmth on those nights, tried to save it up. Others, I would have to muster the courage to approach her as she lay, sullen, in her darkened bedroom, long past dinnertime, and ask her for something to eat, because she had forgotten I was there at all. Some nights she was so angry with me that I didn't bother and I lay awake until exhaustion trumped hunger and I fell asleep. I was used to leaving those kinds of details out. I had practiced since I was little, because every morning, between my dad and the sun, things didn't feel so bad after all. She seemed herself when he was around, so I never told.

But now I was. Sort of.

"The dumb thing was, it was January, and I just ran out in my jammies, following her down the beach."

My voice came out casual, and Tyler laughed softly. But I hugged my arms close to me, because as soon as I said it, the warmth of the evening fell away and I was back in the icy wind, chasing after my mother. Tyler just looked at me, waiting to hear how I found the red piece of glass, so I kept telling.

"Anyway, I went running down the beach after her, but she

was far ahead and I got tired, so I started walking." It was easy to go back to the same details I had changed so many years ago. Really, I had purposely hung back from her. Something I had done earlier in the evening had made her so angry, she'd screamed, then cried, then left me alone in my room. But I tried to walk next to her footprints, so it was almost like we were walking along together. Even that had felt hopeless, though, because the water rushed up and washed them away in front of me as I went along.

"She never turned around and caught you?"

I hesitated, trying to decide in my mind what I really thought. I wanted to believe that she hadn't, that she really didn't know I was there behind her. There had been a moment when she'd paused and I'd thought she'd turned back and seen me. But then she'd kept going.

"No. She thought I was sleeping." My smile was hollow. "She had no idea that her seven-year-old snuck out of the house and was wandering the beach at night."

Tyler nudged me softly with his shoulder. "So you started that habit a long time ago, huh?"

I had been looking out at the water, caught up in my own memory, worlds different from the one I was telling. But now I turned and let my eyes meet his, and I didn't say anything else. Instead I stood up on my tiptoes and kissed him, and when I did, everything that was about to break the surface lingered a moment before it receded into inky blackness, under the weight of his lips on mine.

Tyler slowly pulled his head back, and we stayed there, quiet a moment. "Wow." He rubbed his lips together. "I was right about you not holding back." We laughed until I saw his expression change to one of concern. "Here we go again." He stepped back and shook his head. "I hope your legs are ready to run."

I turned and saw two circles of light in the water, making their way closer to the shore in front of my house. So we ran. Water and lights went by in a blur, and I felt light and fast. We took the back steps to the yard two at a time, and I burst through the kitchen door and threw produce from the refrigerator onto the counter while Tyler grabbed the hose and took up his post rinsing our gear. By the time my dad and Andy tromped up the steps and emptied their lobsters onto the patio, I had caught my breath and was calmly slicing an avocado.

For the rest of the night, Tyler and I weaved our way into each other's paths in small ways—a hand brush while passing a plate, a bump when stepping past each other, a brief second of eye contact when no one else was looking. It was like a game, to see how much we could pass off as chance. The effort of it probably wasn't necessary, though, based on the number of beer bottles lined up on the picnic table. My dad and Andy were on a roll in full glory-days mode, and the stories kept coming as we sat around the low tiled fire ring my dad had bought, surely picturing nights like this one. Still, I liked the idea of trying to keep things with Tyler secret and out of sight. It occupied my mind enough to make me feel like I could just let everything else drift away to be forgotten, the way it had almost been before.

By the end of the night, Andy and my dad had regaled themselves with tales of lifeguarding heroics that had grown in danger and gore each time I'd heard them. Tyler seemed genuinely interested, and won them over by being appropriately impressed, and even adding a few incidents of his own to the mix. At least for the night, he was in the circle of their approval. They included him as one of their own, which made for an easy and comfortable evening. It had cooled down considerably, but the fire warmed my legs as I leaned back in my chair and closed my eyes, listening to their voices and the occasional pop of the coals that remained. When I finally opened my eyes, the tiny twinkle of a star winked through the leaves above me, and I wished that everything could stay like it was, with my mother safely out at sea and the water in my dreams calm and glassy.

Almost instantly she's there. I see the familiar long white skirt and the long blond hair swirling around her. It's just as before, just as it is every time. She walks out slowly but resolutely, unaware of anything else. The frigid wind whips around me and I hug my arms to my chest, trying to hold on to any warmth I can. I've been cold for so long. I see the sharp intake of breath when the water reaches her chest, and I sink back down onto the sand, defeated, knowing what comes next. But this time she doesn't disappear into the swirls of black water.

She turns back to me.

Her eyes are green and clear. When they fall on me, the resolve of her face softens and she looks sorrowful for a moment. I want to look away. I want to run, call my dad. I want to go to her.

It's just the two of us, and she's treading water now, bobbing her chin down into it and then spitting the tangy salt water out, and I'm sure that her lips must be blue, because I'm shivering cold and I haven't touched the water yet.

I hesitate, then walk forward to where the water meets the sand, and when the foam rides up around my ankles, it is me who breathes in sharply, involuntarily, because of the cold.

I'm about to turn around when the water begins to suck back.

I know this sensation, the water pulling all around my feet until it's gone and I am standing on a tiny island. But this time water rushes up from under my feet, where my tiny island should be. It lifts me up and then drops me cruelly into the cold that bites and stings at first touch, and I'm on a rushing river out to sea. Out to my mother.

21

Thick, sullen fog clouded my morning, and the rest of the day wasn't much different. I walked into first period late, had one of Strickland's insults hurled at me, then noticed my usual seat behind Tyler was taken by the blond girl who was also in my English class. She smiled sweetly at me, then leaned forward, tapped his shoulder and whispered something in his ear. He dug a pencil out of his backpack, then looked over at me and rolled his eyes when he handed it back to her. I felt slightly better but didn't have the energy to return any type of gesture.

When the bell rang, I looked around, surprised to see everyone packing up. Tyler walked over. "Hey. What's up? You look all bummed."

I didn't feel like explaining anything. "I'm just tired. I didn't sleep well. Weird dreams, I guess."

Tyler raised his eyebrows. "Oh, *really*? . . . Hope I wasn't the

cause of them. You know, it's been a problem for some girls."
He nodded over at Needy Pencil Girl, who had her hand in her
backpack, texting as she grabbed her notebook with the other
one. She walked past us without so much as a look. I didn't
have a witty response, so I busied myself grabbing my books.
He noticed.

We stepped out the door and stood awkwardly in the breeze-
way, still, in the middle of everyone streaming to their classes.
He put a tentative hand on my shoulder and dipped his head
low, so he was eye level with me. "You sure you're okay? You
seem . . . off."

I watched as the last of the students disappeared into
classrooms, leaving us almost alone. "I'm fine. I gotta go,
though. . . . I can't be late to second." I gave a brief smile,
then took a step backward.

He grabbed my hand. "Lunch, then?"

I winced. "Actually, I promised Ashley I'd have lunch with
her. It's been a little while, and she's got some big thing she
wants to tell me."

For a brief second his shoulders slumped, but he squeezed
my hand and smiled. "All right. Then I'll see you after practice,
if you're not too busy."

"Okay." I nodded, and did my best to smile back. He let
go and took a few steps backward before turning and heading
down the hallway.

I spent the rest of my classes until lunch feeling like a jerk
and hoping Tyler didn't think I was blowing him off. I'd woken
up in a mood that wasn't going away. By the time the bell rang
for lunch, I'd decided to find a place to sit by myself instead of
meeting Ashley. Like clockwork, though, my phone buzzed in
my pocket with a text.

"BIG NEWZ! TABLE ASAP!"

I stood looking at it, about to walk in the other direction, but curiosity got the best of me. Besides, it was hard to be in a bad mood around Ashley.

She had two plastic boxes containing some sort of wraps and cut-up fruit out on the table when I got there, and she waved her bubbly Ashley wave. I sat across from her and smiled, surprised a little at the fact that I'd missed talking to her for a few days. "You didn't need to bring me lunch, you know." She put one hand to her full mouth, then used the other to wave me off. I popped open the box and did my best to sound enthusiastic. "Thank you. So, what's the big news?"

She waved both her hands now, as if that would help her chew faster so she could talk quicker. After a painful-looking swallow, words spilled out, in typical Ashley fashion. "OhmyGodI'msoexcited!" Deep breath in. "This weekend is the opening of the spa at Pelican Crest and my dad is sending me and my mom on Sunday for the full day, and he said I should invite you and your mom too!" Pause for another breath. "It's *the* most luxe spa around, and we can go and have anything—massage, facial, mani-pedi, whatever. And they only use fair-trade organic products, so we'll be doing something good by treating ourselves." She smiled and waited for my enthusiastic answer.

I chewed slowly, trying to buy time, wishing I had just ignored her text and spent lunch alone. We were past the point where I probably should have told her, but there wasn't exactly a simple way to bring up a dead mother. I hadn't totally lied, but looking at Ashley's ridiculously excited smile, I felt guilty knowing that I would now have to. Finally I swallowed and took a sip of water.

"Well?" she asked, waiting.

"Well . . . ," I started, "I don't think we'll be able to make it, Ash." I tried to sound as disappointed as possible.

She dropped her wrap, confounded. "Why?"

I hadn't thought that far ahead yet. I tried to avoid lying to her and went for vague instead. "Um, we already have something planned, some catching-up time, and—"

"Perfect!" She clapped her hands together. "You guys can have a massage together! That's when me and my mom always catch up—"

"No. I don't think it'll work out. We're not like that, my mom and me. We—"

Her face suddenly went serious, and she put a manicured hand on my arm. "Anna, *do not* worry about the money. It's my—well, my dad's—treat! He totally loves being able to give to people who need it." She caught herself, or at least had an inkling that she had said something that could be misunderstood. "You know, like the beautiful women in his life and their friends!" She punctuated this with a nod, clearly happy with herself for her recovery.

I shook my head. "Thanks anyway, but not this time."

Now she looked hurt. And a little ticked off. And kind of pouty. "I thought you'd be excited. I told my mom all about you, and she wants to meet you, and I was excited to meet your mom, and—"

I set down my wrap and looked right at her, sorry for what I was about to say, because I knew it would shock her. "Ash, I don't have anything planned with my mom. . . . She's dead."

She flinched, then leaned in, trying to understand. "What?"

I rubbed my forehead. "She died when I was seven. She drowned. It's just me and my dad." Her face had already fallen into the deeply sad and sympathetic expression I dreaded. "I didn't tell you before because I just wanted a fresh start here, because before I moved, everybody knew about it and . . ." I looked down at my lap, then back up at her, feeling tears well up. "I'm sorry." I bit the inside of my cheek and looked down again.

She was silent, which I had expected. What is anyone supposed to say to something like that? Then her eyes lit up a bit. "You're like a Disney princess!"

It was my turn to flinch. "What?" I asked, wondering if she had heard me right.

"You know," she continued, matter-of-factly. "Ariel, Belle, Cinderella, Jasmine . . . none of them had mothers."

I still wasn't following, but she continued, obviously excited. "When I was little, I used to think that meant that life had to make it up to them, for taking their mothers away, and so that's why they ended up having the whole fairy-tale happily-ever-after magic happen to them. They deserved it more than other girls." She looked at me intently. "Life will make it up to you, Anna."

It was so ridiculous, yet she said it with such confidence and sincerity, I was almost convinced. No one had ever reacted quite like that, but in a way it didn't surprise me with her. I laughed and wiped at my eyes, then breathed in deeply, thankful she had somehow said the exact right thing.

The bell rang, and I went to pick up my half-eaten wrap, but she handed me a mirror instead. "Here. Fix your eyes. In case you see your handsome prince."

I took the mirror and the tissue she handed me and dabbed at my running mascara. "Thank you, Ash."

She smiled at me simply. "That's what friends are for. And

you're still coming. But now I'm ordering you every treatment on the spa menu. Plus products."

"I can't do it that day. We have a race. A big one."

She frowned. "What about if you run, I watch, and *then* we go?"

I considered. It might be nice after the race. "Okay, yeah. That'd be good."

We cleared our table and headed up the path to where it split. She patted my shoulder. "One more period. Then you can try to beat Jillian for once."

I rolled my eyes. "Yeah. That'll be the day."

She gave me a quick hug before we went our separate ways, and I walked slowly, not in the mood for sitting through another class. The hallways were nearly empty now, and quiet, everyone having filed into their last period of the day. A steady breeze of cool air blew up the hill from the ocean, and I looked out over the horizon, which had darkened considerably since I'd come outside.

I wasn't going to seventh period. I walked past my class-room, then turned the corner to the back of campus, where I had seen a massive elm tree with branches like an umbrella.

It was good to be alone. Even better that I was missing class. I leaned my back against the elm tree's knobby bark and looked up through the leaves that rustled above me in the breeze. The sky was a pale slab of marble now, white and gray with darker veins running through it. It had yet to spill a drop, but it felt like rain today, and smelled like it too. I closed my eyes and breathed it in, finally relaxing a little.

"Mind if I share the tree?"

I opened my eyes to Jillian standing above me with one hip cocked out, her hand resting on it. I shrugged. "Sure."

She sat down without saying anything, settled her back into the bark of the tree, and took out her iPod. I cleared my throat and looked around, fairly sure that she didn't want a conversation. Maybe she'd woken up in a mood too.

Jillian put in both of her earbuds and was scrolling through her music. She wore jeans, a tank top, and the same calm expression she always did, whether she was kicking my butt or just barely holding me off. I sighed loudly. "So . . . what class are you ditching?"

She took out one earbud and turned around to look at me. "Huh? Oh, Leadership." She smiled. "Ironic, right? What about you? Why are you out here?"

I twirled the stem of a leaf between my fingers. "English. I couldn't make myself do it today. Too much other stuff on my mind."

She nodded. "Yeah. Same here." When she looked down at the iPod in her hand again, I figured our conversation had run its course, and I let my eyes wander out over the field. Out of the corner of my eye, though, I saw her foot tap a few times, then she turned back to me. "My sister died two years ago today."

She said it like it was a normal thing to say, then picked at the grass next to her before looking back up at me and shrugging. "Guess that's why I'm out here."

I kept my face steady and looked her in the eye. Two things I wished people could do with me when they found out. Neither one of us said anything for a moment. I figured that if she had brought it up, she might want to talk about it. "Were you close with her?"

At first she looked at me like I was crazy, then eased off and nodded. "Yeah. We were close. We did everything together. She was a runner too. Faster than me, actually."

She plucked a blade of grass and rolled it between her fingers, watching the end spin. I watched it too, and then, because it seemed like the right thing to do, I asked her what nobody ever really asked me.

"What happened?"

Her fingers stopped, and she looked at me for a long moment before picking another piece and beginning again. "We went to this party together. She always brought me along so she could make me drive home if she got drunk, which she always did." She laughed softly. "She was the only person I knew who could get wasted at night and set records the next day."

She paused and swept her eyes over the field, and I waited for the rest. Her smile faded slowly before she started again.

"I never drank. I held her hair when she got sick, snuck her in the back door, and lied to our parents when she couldn't. Except that night. We got into a fight over something stupid, because she was drunk, and I left. I was so pissed, I just left her there to deal with it herself for once." She looked at me like she'd just confessed something horrible, and I wanted to tell her I understood her more than she knew.

"She left the party, I guess to walk home, and some other drunk girl who was driving home swerved off the road and hit her with her car. And then the driver took off and left her there. And I was at home, lying to my parents for my sister, while she was out in the road, dying."

I could see the guilt wrapped around her tight, and I knew there was nothing I could say to loosen it. But I tried anyway, because if I really thought about it, it was the thing I most wanted to hear myself.

"It wasn't your fault. There was no way you could have—"

"I know that." She cut me short in a flicker of emotion, then almost as quickly regained her composure. "Sorry. Everyone has told me that, and logically it's probably true." She shrugged. "I just don't think I'll ever stop wondering about the what-ifs, though. You know? It's just shitty and unfair. . . ."

She trailed off again, and I shifted my weight. I focused hard on her. Avoided the fact that I felt the same way. "But you still run. Isn't that hard sometimes? Because that was a thing you did together?"

"No." She turned to me. "Running is the place I feel closest to her, where I can get away from the rest of it."

I thought about my own running, which I'd been doing for a long time. "I get it. It's the one time I can forget about everything and just go. Hard."

She laughed softly, then sat up straight, and I could tell the conversation was about to shift. "I knew it. You always run like you're running away from something." She zipped her iPod into her backpack. "It's good you're up for going hard, because today is mile repeats. Four of them, at six-minute pace."

I took a deep breath and pushed it out as we stood up. "Oh, God."

"It won't hurt that bad . . . when we're done." She threw her backpack over her shoulder. "I can promise you this, you won't have anything else in your mind besides the pain we're about to feel. I think that's why coach decided to do them today, in my honor. Or Krista's. She used to kick everyone's ass in these."

"Well, guess it's up to you to carry on the tradition." We headed toward the locker room.

Jillian raised an eyebrow and smiled. "Yeah? We'll see."

She was right. About the pain being the only thing in my mind. After the first mile my lungs burned and my legs quivered from the effort. I crossed the line at the same time as Jillian, and after our talk this afternoon, I did it more out of wanting to be a friend to her than feeling competitive. We jogged the next lap without talking, working on getting our breath and heart rates back to normal. At the starting line for the second mile, we shook out our legs and waited for Coach Martin's whistle. I took off hard, getting a jump on her at first. She caught me quickly though, and just as she did, I felt the first fat drop of rain land on my cheek. By the time we rounded the turn and headed into the third lap, the sky opened up on us with an intensity that I relished.

Time shifted and I ceased to think about anything but breathing and pushing my legs forward through the rain that blurred my vision and hid the tears that welled up, hot and fierce. And it hurt like nothing else, but as I looked at Jillian from the corner of my eye, I felt like I wasn't alone in what I was running from. And that, at least, was a comfort.

22

"EAT PASTA, RUN FASTA!"

The peppy banner hung over Jillian's dining room table a few days later. Her mom had volunteered to host "team night" at her house a night before the Breakers Invitational tradition and had gone all out—complete with enough spaghetti, garlic bread, and salad to feed all the teams in the meet. I watched her flit around us, winking as she heaped more noodles onto our plates, laughing heartily when we said we were full, and running Jillian around with a million tiny requests that I could see were wearing on her.

When she asked Jillian, for the third time, to see if anyone wanted more garlic bread, it was clear she'd pushed a button. Jillian took her mom by the shoulders, forcing her to be still a moment, and said, as calmly as she could, "*Mom*. You need to relax. We're all fine. If anyone needs anything else, it's all out here on the counter for them to get." She swept her arm over the spread. Beth took a deep breath, pressed her lips together, and nodded, before turning to find another detail that needed attending. The brief little exchange made me wonder if her constant, smiling busyness was natural, or if it was one of the ways Beth dealt with the loss of her other daughter. Judging by Jillian's strained mood, I guessed it was the latter. And I felt for her, having to deal with her own grief along with her mom's. It was a lot to stand up under.

Nobody else seemed to notice amidst the chatter and laughter of the whole team at one table. Even Coach Martin had come, and for once he let down his serious-coach demeanor to laugh with us and eat a ridiculous amount of spaghetti. After three helpings courtesy of Jill's mom, he wiped his mouth with a napkin and stood up at the head of the table, clearing his throat to get our attention. When our forks clinked down onto our plates, and the chatter died down, he clapped his hands together.

"Ladies, ladies, ladies. First off, we owe a big thank you to Jillian's mom for this feast here. It's a lot of work she put in to feed you girls, so let's give her a big hand." We all did, and the smile that spread over Beth's face was genuinely happy. Coach went on. "Now. Let's talk a little business about tomorrow." Feigned groans rippled around the table, and he waved a dismissive hand. "Tomorrow's meet isn't a league meet, but I want you to treat it like it is. The team that wins the Breakers Invitational wins the sponsorship of the Newport Running Club, which means brand-new uniforms, shoes, and money enough for a cushy trip to Mt. Sac, when that race comes around. So we want this one. Bad." He looked over at me and Jillian. "Jill, you and Anna are gonna lead. Keep everyone together as much as possible, and work the hills like I know you two can, okay?" We both nodded. "All right. Now let's finish up, help Mrs. Matthews get her kitchen clean, and then get home and get some rest."

Coach Martin wasn't one for big speeches, but he got his point across. After helping with the dishes, I left Jillian's more than a little nervous about being charged with the task of leading the team.

By the time I got home, I was nervous in an entirely different way. The tingly, butterfly, electric way. Every day since the beginning of the week, Tyler had come down after practice in the evening when the sun was setting, and we'd wait for my dad to do his patrol lap before we headed, barefoot, onto the darkened beach. Once the lights of the truck bumped up the hill to patrol the parking lots above, the night, the beach, and the cottages were ours. In a week's time we'd made our way through several of them, with Tyler as my personal guide and me more than happy to go along listening to his random bits of history and stories about the cove.

I checked the clock when I came in from dinner and was relieved I had a few minutes before he was supposed to meet me. Enough time at least for a spritz of perfume and a mint. Once freshened up, I sat on the couch and waited for the now familiar sound of his flip-flops coming up our front steps. The sun had just set, but it was darker than usual because of the clouds that had moved in. A storm was supposed to hit hard by the next evening, but from the looks of the sky, it was gonna be early. I hoped, after all the buildup this week, the race wouldn't be rained out. I was nervous, but I'd stored up a lot in the last few weeks that I needed to let loose. And for now, at least, running seemed to be the best way to do it.

Tyler's knock interrupted my thoughts. I hadn't heard the shuffle of his feet, but he stood silhouetted against the sky when I opened the door.

"Hey." He stepped into me and smiled. "You smell good."

I stood on tiptoes and kissed him lightly. "You smell like a pool."

"You love it."

"I don't know about *love,* but it's growing on me." I took a step back. "Where to tonight?"

He glanced out the door. "It's looking like it's gonna rain soon. You wanna stick close?"

"Yeah, we probably should. Let me just get my sweater."

We sat on the gritty deck of the lifeguard tower in front my house, feet propped up on the railing. A layer of clouds hung low in the sky, illuminated by the lights below, and a set wave pounded the sand, exploding in a white line down the length of the beach. At the rocks it sprayed high into the air, then pulled back in preparation for another surge.

"Man, I'm glad we never got this much swell this summer. That'd be a sketchy rescue out there in waves like that."

The next wave thundered down onto the rocks, erupting white water into the sky. "My dad's got some scary stories about rock rescues."

"I know." He smiled. "I heard the best ones last weekend."

I laughed under my breath. "They get like that when they're together, him and Andy. That's what they've always done . . . for as long as I can remember."

Tyler nodded slowly, like he was thinking about something, then he looked over at me. "Andy's like family to you guys, huh?"

Another wave—this one smaller than the others—washed over the rocks, and I swallowed, suddenly wary of where our conversation could go. But then I steered it in that direction. "Yeah. He's like family. Ever since my mom died. He's always been there for us." I looked down at my hands, surprised at what I'd said. I'd wanted nothing more than to avoid mentioning or thinking about her since Tyler had put his hand to my cheek and kissed me that night. And now there she was again.

Tyler glanced over his shoulder, toward her cottage. "Is it hard for you, or him, to live here?" I hadn't realized he could know it had been hers. But then again, it made sense. He knew about all the other ones.

I watched another wave explode on the rocks. "Not any harder than it was living at the beach where she drowned." It came out sounding harsher than I'd meant it to, and I cleared my throat and sat up straight. "I'm sorry. I didn't mean to sound . . ."

Tyler put a warm hand on my leg. "You didn't. Don't worry about it." He sat up and listened. "What you should worry about is that your dad must have hidden cameras around here or something." He shook his head. "Damn."

I looked around, confused at first, but then I saw the bump of headlights flashing over the sand. "You've got to be kidding me."

"Nope." He scooted toward the ladder. "We should go."

"Wait a sec." I had to smile at his nervousness. "You just got here. Stay. I'll pretend like I was on a walk or something, then I'll come back."

Tyler shook his head. "Nah, I should go. I got that game tomorrow anyway. But you go first." He pushed himself back against the front wall of the tower and leaned back so I could climb over him. I paused when I got to his lap, and he looked at me, serious. "Anna. If you ever want to, we could go in there together. Your mom's old place, I mean." He shrugged. "Just . . . if you're curious. I'd go with you."

I didn't want to think about it. "Maybe one day." I gave him a quick kiss, knowing I never would, then climbed over him to the ladder.

"Think about it." He leaned down and kissed me once more. "Good luck in your race. I'll call you when I get back from the game."

"Okay. I don't think we'll dive or anything with the storm that's coming in, but we sometimes do pizza night when we can't do Poke-N-Eat. I'll let you know." Tyler nodded and leaned back into the tower's shadow while I jumped down into the sand, took a breath, and walked out into my dad's low beams.

He pulled around me and rolled down his window, looking at me with furrowed eyebrows. "Hey, hon. What're you doing out here?"

I shrugged. "I needed some fresh air. Thought I'd check out the swell that's coming in." Another wave hit with a low rumble. "It's getting big out here tonight."

He looked out toward the water. "Yeah. It's supposed to keep building until tomorrow night. Don't think we'll be doing any diving."

Another wave pounded the rocks. "Yeah. I wouldn't want to be out there anytime soon."

A woman dispatcher's voice crackled over the radio in the truck, and my dad turned it up and cocked his head to the side to listen. Something about the upper parking lot. He responded in code, the only part of which I recognized was his badge number. He leaned his elbow out the window. "I gotta go up there. Why don't you go on into the house?"

I nodded and turned to go, then paused. "Dad?"

"Yeah?"

I shook my head. "Nothing . . . I'll see you in the morning. Good night."

He stuck his arm out and rested a heavy hand on my head. "Night, Anna. I love you. Now go back in and get to bed. You got your big race tomorrow." I nodded and turned again to head back to home. As I did, the forceful clap of water on rocks made me jump before I jogged up the sand to our house, suddenly cold.

Once inside, I watched my dad's headlights move north up the beach, slicing through the darkness in front of them. And then, like they always did, my eyes wandered over to the beach cottage. Between what Tyler and my dad had told me, it sounded like my great-grandma had been there until the end, when they'd all had to leave. Which meant my mother's room had been too. I sat for a moment, considering Tyler's offer to take me in. When I grabbed the spare flashlight from the charger, I told myself I'd feel better if I looked inside just once, by myself.

23

The padlock was rusted through. I wrapped my hand around the crumbling metal and yanked down hard. It fell to the dirt with a clunk, and the door inched open. I looked around to make sure no one had seen, then took a deep breath and stepped over the doorway. The now-familiar smell of damp wood and stale air hung heavy around me in the darkness and sat utterly still, in contrast to my heart, which jumped and kicked in my chest. I hesitated, then clicked on the flashlight, keeping it pointed at the ground. Mouse pellets, dirt, and wood shavings covered the floor beneath my feet, and dark wood paneled all of the walls.

My gut reaction was to get out—back into air I could breathe and back to the place I had kept myself in for so long, where my mother was just another one of my childhood memories that had long since grown hazy and surreal. But I had crossed the threshold, and now something in me forced my feet forward. I swung the flashlight in a slow arc around the edges of the room, which had probably once been the living area.

To my left I could see an old stove through a small doorway. Beyond that lay a short hallway with another door off to the right. I crept past the kitchen, then stopped and peeked into a tiny bathroom. A dry toilet stood in the center, surrounded by pieces of broken tiles and rusty pipe. As I turned to go on, the thick threads of a cobweb stretched across my face, and I swatted frantically at them, dropping my flashlight in the process.

It thudded onto the wood floor, rolling loudly before coming to a stop against the wall. There, in the narrow shaft of light, I saw the bottom step of a staircase that angled up almost vertically. Up until that moment it hadn't felt much different from the other cottages in their broken-down state. I stared at the dust particles orbiting one another in the light, and I knew. If there was any space in the house that had been hers, that could possibly have some remnant of my mother in it, it would be up the stairs.

The first step sagged under my weight, so I crept up slowly, keeping my feet to the edges of the steps, testing them first before putting my weight fully on them. I was concentrating on this pattern of placing my feet, and then lifting my weight, when I reached the top step and finally looked up.

It was visibly lighter in this room. Not only because the walls were all painted white, but because of the large window that looked out directly onto the rocky tide pools that drew so many people, including myself. Just beyond them, a boat, probably out for lobster, sat beyond the breaking waves. Its blue-white light waved and bobbed gently over the shiny black surface and splashed a bright pool around the hull.

The image it created looked like a painting. I stepped back and realized why. The frame around the window was wide with detailed corners, a frame around the perfect canvas. I imagined how the picture in the center must continually change in color and texture, through seasons and weather.

Your mother was a brilliant artist.

I stepped closer, keeping the light as low as I could. To the side of the window a small door opened out to the balcony I had been so intrigued by. My hand reached for the crystal knob, then stopped short as a dark shape on the window frame caught my eye. Cautiously I raised my light up to it and brushed away a layer of dirt to reveal what lay beneath.

It was a tail.

A curved tail that tapered and ended in two curling tips. My eyes followed the graceful lines upward and found the woman's body and waving hair that I knew would be there. I stood on my tiptoes and reached my hand up to the top corner of the window frame, then ran it down the length of it, squatting when I reached the bottom. Dirt and salty film coated my fingertips, but I didn't wipe them off.

I continued with my hand, along the bottom of the window frame, wiping away the dust, then up the other side. Faded mermaids, beautiful in their curves and waves, swam among rocks and coral in an underwater garden. When I got to the top, I had to move on raised toes, wiping the grime away with each step. No swimming figures bordered the top of the window. Instead there were three words, scrawled in faded paint. I stepped back and shined my light on them.

BEAUTY, GRACE, STRENGTH.

I stared at them, afraid to breathe, then repeated them in

my head. *Beauty. Grace. Strength.* No recognition or memory came to me, no special significance behind them. She had placed her brush on that window frame, and with delicate strokes had left something of herself, something meaningful to her that I didn't understand. That I might never understand. Were those the things she valued most? The things she wished she'd had? Things she wanted to pass on?

I stood rooted to the sagging wood floor and switched off the flashlight. Then I sat down and cried.

She was all around me, everywhere I turned, from the moment we had arrived. And still . . . she wasn't. I had fooled myself into thinking I felt some connection to this place. There it was, right in front of me. Her art. Three words. And nothing else.

I wiped my eyes, hard, wishing I hadn't let myself think there had even been a possibility of anything else. She had left me alone in the dark long ago, and this time was no different. I put my head down on my knees, and my red moonglass slipped out of the edge of my shirt and swung back and forth on its chain before coming to a stop, dangling in the dark, inches from my face.

I closed my hand around it and felt the same smooth contours that I had for the last nine years, since the night she died. A piece of sea glass. That's what she left me. I knew now that she had dropped it for me to find.

Some walks, when we combed the beach for glass, I would get discouraged when I didn't find anything at first. It always seemed that as soon as I would want to turn around and quit looking, a piece of glass would magically appear in front of me in the sand, giving me just enough reason to keep searching.

I had heard her tell my dad as they lay next to each other on our beach blanket one afternoon, soaking up the sun, that she dropped them for me to find. A few feet away I carved a tunnel into my sand castle, and I decided to walk far away from her from then on, to see if I could find them all by myself. And so when I picked up the red piece that night, and looked up and down the beach, bursting to tell her, I believed I had found it all by myself.

Because she'd been walking out into the water.

24

I squinted through the morning drizzle, watching the town car make its way down the hill. Ashley had arranged for me to be picked up and taken to the race so we could go to the spa afterward. Between the rain and a sleepless night, I'd gotten up ready to bail on both, but I didn't want to have to tell Jillian that I wasn't running, or Ashley that I was canceling, so I'd forced myself into my uniform and packed a bag for the spa.

The car stopped directly in front of me, and the driver hopped out. He jogged around to open the door I was already reaching for.

"Thank you. You didn't have to get out in the rain, though." I dropped my hand and took a step back, allowing him to open the door. As he did, Ashley leaned her head out.

"Hiieee! Get in, get in!" She patted the seat and scooted over to make room. I sat down. "Are you ready for your race?

And the spa? You are going to love this day." The door closed, and she chattered on excitedly. "Sugar glow scrub, ocean algae body wrap . . ." I watched the turbulent gray water as we pulled away, still full of the empty melancholy I'd felt the night before, in my mother's room.

"Anna? You okay? . . . You listening?"

"Yeah. Sorry. That all sounds great. I'm just a little nervous for this race," I lied as we made our way down the highway toward the school.

She bumped my shoulder. "Oh, don't be nervous. You and Jillian are, like, the best runners we have. You'll do fine! Is your dad coming? Or Tyler? We could make a little cheering section."

"No, Tyler has a water polo game, and my dad got called out early this morning for a missing boat or something. The waves are huge right now."

"Oh. Well, don't worry. I'll cheer for ya."

I nodded and turned back to the window, watching the gray streak past me. "Thanks, Ash. I appreciate it."

When we pulled up to the course, I spotted Jillian right away. She wore a red plastic poncho over her uniform and stood stretching while Coach Martin went over something on his clipboard. I felt the slightest bit better, knowing we'd be running together and that I'd have to go all out. I needed to today.

We stopped in front of them, and Ashley squeezed my leg. "Good luck! I have Gatorade and snacks for when you finish. I'm gonna wait in here until the race starts. Tell them all I said good luck!"

"All right." I opened the door and stepped out into the cool, wet air.

Coach looked over. "You got a chauffeur service now, Ryan?" He tossed a small plastic package to me. "Put this on. It'll keep you warm before you get started."

I opened the snap and shook out the poncho, then slid it over me. "Thanks."

He turned and put his hands to his mouth. "Coast High! I need you guys over here." Over his shoulder I saw red ponchos move through the crowd of runners and tents.

Jillian walked over. "Hey. Hope you're ready to kick some ass today, cuz we've got serious competition." She motioned with her head to a blue team gathered beneath a pop-up tent. "Their number one has the record for this course."

"Great." I tried to joke, but it was forced. "No pressure or anything." I didn't want to be there. I didn't want to go to the spa, and I didn't want to be at home, either. I wanted to go far away from everything, somewhere my mom had never been or left.

The night before, I'd sat there on her bedroom floor for who knows how long, and something in me shifted. From the emptiness of the room and the sharp absence of her, anger rose in me. I'd never let myself be angry with her before, but now I couldn't push it away.

Coach Martin clapped his hands together forcefully. "Okay, ladies, this is it. I know the conditions aren't the best, but get over that. I need your heads in this race. Jill, you and Anna are going for one and two." He looked over the rest of the girls. "We need to take as many of the top ten spots as we can, so stick together and go hard. It only hurts for three miles." He put his hand out in the center of us, and we stacked ours on top. "Coast Breakers! Go!"

Our tight circle disintegrated as we backed up and shed our

ponchos. We walked as a group to the starting line, where runners from six or eight different teams jumped up and down, rubbing their arms to keep warm. The official blew his whistle, and we reigned in our nervous energy enough to listen as he went over the course. We had an advantage, having trained on it, but its hills still made for a brutal race. A race that my head was definitely not in. The race official finished up his instructions, then walked the line, making sure we were all behind it. When he got to the other side, coaches raised their stopwatches out in front of them, thumbs hovering over the start buttons. The official held the gun high above his head and yelled the words that shot adrenaline through me every time. "Runners! Take your mark!"

The sharp crack of the gun sent us off in a crowd of elbows and feet jostling for space. Jillian was a step ahead of me, and I focused only on staying with her. Within a few seconds the group thinned out as we took our positions with the top runners from the other teams. And then the rain started.

It wasn't a drop or two that made you wonder if it was really going to rain or not, building until you knew. It was like someone had taken a knife to the clouds and let loose everything in them. Instinctively we all put our heads down as we tromped over the dirt trail that would be mud within minutes.

I thought of my dad then, out in the rain, looking for a boat that had been stupid enough to go out, despite the storm warnings, and I felt ill.

My dad.

The night she left, while I sat huddled in a blanket with my grandmother in our warm house, he pulled on his own dive gear and went out into the icy water to search for her. And later, while I slept, helicopters flooded light down into the black chop of winter and radioed to him that they saw nothing. And finally, as I bent in my dream to touch a hand that reached out of calm blue water, she disappeared into the cold blackness of the night, leaving behind only swirls of questions and ripples of guilt. The thought of him out there looking that night, when I knew what had happened, pricked holes in my chest, and I felt my legs waver. Jillian glanced over.

"You slip?" She was breathing hard, red-cheeked.

"No, I—"

"Come on," she huffed. "You're slowing down."

I squinted and tried to match her stride as rivulets of water flowed into my eyes.

"Come on. Run away from whatever it is. We got a hill coming up."

We both breathed hard, and water splashed up our legs now with each step. I couldn't. I couldn't leave it behind or run away anymore. I'd been the reason life wasn't what she wanted it to be. She may have chosen it in the beginning, but the night she drowned herself, she made another choice. One that didn't consider me, or my dad, or what we might live with afterward.

I stopped running. Just stopped. Right in the middle of the trail.

Immediately two runners passed me, and Jillian looked over her shoulder, completely taken aback. She didn't have time to ask any questions, though. She turned and kept running, looking back once, in time to see me walk off the course.

I inhaled slowly and willed back tears that sprung, hot, to my eyes. A short distance away I could see Ashley's car in the parking lot, steam rising from the exhaust. Our tent was empty, and I figured everyone was out along the course, watching the second mile by now.

I needed to get away.

When I opened the town car door, the driver turned around, surprised. "That was quick. How'd you do?"

"I need to go home. I don't feel well. Could you take me?" I was still breathing hard, water running down my face.

He looked around, confused. "Where's Ashley?"

"I think she's out on the course somewhere. But I really need to go home. Could you take me real quick? Please? I'll call her and explain when I get home." I knew I'd owe her an apology later, but I needed to leave.

He gave one last look around, then nodded once. "Hop in."

25

Outside the town car's window angry clouds loomed as far as I could see, and rain fell in translucent walls. I sat silently, but felt the driver's eye on me in the rearview mirror.

"Not feeling well, huh?" I didn't answer. "There's always something going around. I tell ya what, though. You go home, get some sleep, then drink some yerba maté. You'll feel much better. Ashley got me started on the stuff months ago, and I haven't been sick since."

I nodded politely and tried to smile.

"Actually"—he reached across the front seat—"I've got some you can take with you. Here." He handed back a brown bag, then looked at me again in the mirror. "It's wonder stuff. Great for the memory, too, I read somewhere."

"Thanks." I looked down at the bag in my hands. I didn't need any help with my memory, though. That was crystal clear.

✳

She had paused as I'd trailed behind her in the wind. And
when she did, I froze, suddenly afraid of how angry she would
be that I had followed her. She paused and she looked out at
the ocean, her hair and skirt whipping around behind her. And
in silhouette she was beautiful, like a mermaid out of water,
and all I wanted to do was make her happy again, so I looked
down to the sand at my feet, hoping to find a piece of glass for
her. And it was there, all by itself, next to the vague imprint
of her foot. She had walked right over a piece of moonglass,
a perfect delicate triangle with smoothed edges. I bent into
the wind to pick it up, and when I held it up to the moonlight, it glowed a deep red. And I ran. Ran to show her what
I had found, because I knew she would pick me up and spin
me around and tell me I had found a treasure. She wouldn't
be mad once I showed her, so I yelled, ecstatic, as my bare
feet slapped over cold, wet sand. "Mommy! Mommy! I found
moonglass!" It would make her so happy.

And then I slowed down, confused and out of breath, until
I stood digging my toes into the sand as I watched.

She stood knee-deep in the water, and her skirt clung to her
legs. On sunny days we would sometimes wade in up to our
knees and peer down in between the breaking waves to look
for pieces of glass being tumbled around underwater. But she
wasn't looking down. She wasn't searching for glass. She was
staring straight out at the ocean, like she didn't even feel the
cold or the wind.

I watched, confused.

I watched her walk out there. And the wind howled around
me, and my toes went numb, and I watched. She loved to
swim. She was the one who could coax me into the water

when the sound of the waves scared me onto the sand. But on that night I didn't follow her. I watched from the shore as she waded out into the frigid black water.

She didn't flinch or turn back when it reached her chest. She didn't raise her arms up to keep them from the cold. She didn't swim.

She just walked out.

I stood there who knows how long, watching the spot where she went under, waiting. I didn't take my eyes off it, because I didn't want to miss her when she came back up. I would surprise her there on the beach, and she would be so proud of my red piece of moonglass—

"Miss? If you like, I could walk you the rest of the way to your cottage."

We were parked at a sign that read FOOT TRAFFIC ONLY at the entrance to the park. The driver turned around, waiting for me to answer. Behind him rain streamed down the windshield and wind whipped the palm trees, threatening to break them apart.

"No. Thanks. I'll walk."

He looked concerned. "You sure you're all right?"

I leveled my eyes at him and smiled. "I'm fine. Really. Tell Ashley I'm sorry and that I'll call her."

He faced forward and eyed the dirt road that was now a minefield of puddles, before turning back to me. "Then take the umbrella, at least. And get into dry clothes as soon as you get home."

"I will." I nodded. "Thank you." I opened the door and then the umbrella, waved good-bye, and stepped out into the wind and rain like I didn't feel a thing.

As soon as I rounded the corner, I collapsed the umbrella and let the rain fall hard onto my face. It pricked my cheeks, then ran down like tears I wouldn't let fall. She had seen me, I knew. And then she had left me, alone, shivering cold, waiting for her to come back.

Now a burst of white water on sand reverberated against the cottages, and I watched as the ocean, wild and angry, lined up waves, one after another. I gave up waiting for her a long time ago, and that was fine until we got here. Until she came back, like everything in the ocean does.

Another wave thundered down, and this time I felt it in my chest. Up ahead I could make out the blurry outline of the shack, which stood, cold and empty, in the dim afternoon. I forced my eyes away from it and up to our front window, where light warmed the room. Maybe dad would be back from his rescue, stretched out on the couch in his sweats, reading a book. He'd look up, smile, and give me a hard time for being soaked. He'd tell me to hop into the shower to warm up. Then he'd ask me if I wanted hot chocolate, mainly because he'd want some too but would never make it just for himself.

He had made it for me that night. After I'd heard him yelling over the wind while I sat huddled against it. The wetness of the sand had soaked up through my pajama bottoms and chilled me so that my entire body shook and twitched. But I squeezed my hand tight around my moonglass, and I lifted my head when I heard him close by. He pulled his work jacket off and scooped me up, protecting me from the cold and the wind and the flashlights swinging around with voices behind them, now calling only my mother's name. He warmed me under blankets, then made hot chocolate that stood untouched while he held on to me tight and asked, over and over, "Did you see where Mommy went, Anna? Did she go into the water?" When I finally nodded, he went silent and stayed that way until my grandma arrived to take over.

I stopped at the end of the road and stood in the rain between the shack and our lighted window. And I hated her. I hated her for leaving us, and I hated her for coming back.

I dropped the umbrella into the mud, then checked our window again before kicking off my shoes. The rocks were barely discernible beneath the high tide and chaotic surf, but I kept my eyes on them as I bent my head to undo the clasp of the necklace. Then I walked over pitted sand, pummeled by raindrops, straight out to the rocks. Calm, like she had been.

A gust of wind smacked me on the back, and rain pierced my clinging jersey, but I only felt the weight of the moon-glass, squeezed tight in my hand. And now the weight of it wasn't enough to keep me searching for another little glimmer. Finally I was finished with her, like she had been with me. She could have it back.

On the outer edge of the rocks, a wall of water stood up tall before it pitched forward and blasted them, sending spray high into the air, like rain falling upward. Frothy water churned and swirled around my ankles when I stepped onto the first rock, and I breathed in sharply, because of the cold. My feet found their way over craters in the rocks and the jagged edges of mussel shells, to a place that felt far enough out to leave her behind.

I uncurled my fingers. Looked at it one last time. Then resolve clenched my hand around the glass, and I chucked it, as hard as I could, into the oncoming wall of water. The force I threw it with shocked me. I saw the tiny glint of red disappear into the face of the wave at the same moment I realized what was about to happen.

I didn't have time to be shocked when the wave hit me.

The thunder of waves, the pounding of the rain, all of it went quiet. It was replaced by a muffled rushing, angry and chaotic, that whipped me around. I wasn't unfamiliar with the sensation, having been tossed by waves more times than I could remember. I held my breath, even when I felt my body land with a dull thud on the rocks, then bounce over them in the violent water, all limbs and odd angles, completely out of control. My toes scraped rock, and I kicked off hard and broke the surface, barely in time to get a breath before I felt the pull backward, back over the jagged edges of the tide pools. Then, the next onslaught. This one hit with the force of a wall tumbling down onto me, but it was instantly stilled by the muffled crack of my head, which sent sparks of light bursting in front of my eyes. I didn't feel the edges of the rocks. I almost didn't feel the sensation of moving at all.

Eighty-seven seconds.

Every spring, when I was little, I sat in the back of the lifeguard headquarters and listened to my dad read to a new batch of rookie guards a passage from *The Perfect Storm* about the stages of drowning. It said eighty-seven seconds is the break point. The urge not to breathe underwater is so strong that your body does it automatically, but only until the break point. After eighty-seven seconds the need for oxygen forces the body to take an involuntary breath, even if it's a mouthful of water. I remembered this because each time I heard it, I wondered if she had lasted that long, if she'd had that long to change her mind.

I clenched my jaw tight and, with all the will in me, forced my eyes open in the churning, murky water. I saw no light to go by, nothing to give me any point of reference. There was nothing but gray, with blackness creeping in around the edges. I must have been moving, still tumbling, but I no longer felt it. Darkness closed in further, leaving only a tiny circle of gray in front of me. In my mind I screamed, fought, anything not to be like her. Dark closed in even faster. My lungs ached; my limbs tossed around me, deadened; and my body hung suspended while my mind fought every one of those eighty-seven seconds.

26

Thin, brittle arms dragged me from the water. They shook with the effort, and their owner grunted as my heels dug two wavy paths in the wet sand. Pain ripped around my head in a quick lap when I tried to look up. My eyes felt heavy again, and I struggled to focus on the rolling horizon that bumped and bounced in front of me.

The arms laid me down gently, and shaking hands moved around my neck, searching. They settled on a tender spot and waited, still. Then, I felt a cold hand on my head and the presence of someone close to my face, listening. I tried to form words, to say that I was here, and when I did, I was suddenly aware of the bitter salt water that pooled in the cavity between my nose and mouth. I coughed and sputtered, trying to spit it out, and the hands rolled me onto my side so that I could. Another wave of pain shot around my head, and I spat onto the sand.

"Go on. Get it out." The voice was tired, out of breath.

I forced my eyes open, then blinked hard to focus on the objects that swung and clinked gently in front of me. Their owner didn't move, and once they stilled, I saw what they were.

Crosses.

"Do you know what day it is?" He looked from my head to my eyes, back and forth.

This time I got the words out. Barely. "Sunday. . . . You're here on Sundays." Cautiously I lifted my eyes to his face, and I was surprised by what I saw. He wore a faded red bandana around a scalp that was buzzed close, showing only the faintest trace of silver stubble, which mirrored the unshaven skin of his face. His skin was tanned to a deep brown and worn, no doubt the result of hours of penance spent under the sun. It was his eyes, though, that pulled me out of my haze. They were piercing blue against the backdrop of so much gray. And so sad. He didn't hold my gaze long before he looked down at the sand between us and finally started to catch his breath.

After a long moment he spoke, without looking at me. "You've hit your head. We should call help."

I started to shake my head, but stopped abruptly because of the pain. "I'm all right. My dad's right up there." I motioned more with my eyes than anything else, but he got the point. Still, he didn't say anything. He seemed lost in his thoughts for a minute, then he looked from me to our cottage and back again.

"I'll take you there." And he inched himself up, until he was hunched next to me. It seemed his natural posture, and so I was surprised, both at the motion and the strength involved in it, when he pulled me to my feet and slung my arm over his frail shoulders. And slowly, without speaking, we made our way up the beach through the mist.

✳

Inside, muffled rain on the roof was the only sound. Our cottage was empty. Warm, but empty. The crawling man lowered me carefully into my green chair and covered me with a blanket. Then, almost against his will, he collapsed onto the couch. And we sat there and let it sink in. I had almost drowned right in front of my house. My dad would have come home and I would have been gone. History would have repeated itself.

But it was Sunday.

I looked directly at the crawling man, who now folded his arms over his chest and his crosses. He had been there. "You saved me." It was somewhere between a question and a statement. Whatever it was, it brought his blue eyes to mine briefly before they scanned the water outside the window.

He nodded vaguely.

Again we were quiet, but my thoughts were not. How had he seen me? How had I *not* seen him? How in the world had this frail old man dragged me from the water? I had only ever seen him crawl. But he had saved me. I kept my eyes on the water because it seemed he would be more comfortable that way. Waves crashed down, surreal, over the rocks he had plucked me from, and I spoke without knowing really what I was going to say.

"Do you believe things happen for a reason? Or do you think everything is just coincidence—that out there you were just in the right place at the right time?"

More than a few beats passed, and I wondered if he had heard me. But then he inhaled deeply, dropped his head, and spoke into his lap. "I don't know the answer to that." Cautiously his eyes came up to meet mine. "I've been asking myself that question for the last twenty years." An eternity to crawl the beach, trying to answer that question.

"And you?" He motioned gently with his head, toward the window. "Seems you were in the wrong place at the wrong time out there on those rocks. And that you know better."

Now it was me who avoided his eyes. I felt the absence of weight around my bare neck and consciously fought the urge to bring my hand to where my moonglass had rested. Behind the realization of what I had done, the guilt and anger from the moment when I had unclasped the necklace lined up again like the sets of waves outside, ready to come crashing down. I shook my head and laughed, joyless.

"Or maybe I was meant to be out there. Maybe I'm just as selfish and thoughtless as my mother was." It came out bitter, and he flinched, almost imperceptibly, before his forehead creased. I looked at her cottage. "Or maybe I'm why she was that way."

We both sat quietly, and I could feel the crawling man considering what I had said. He sat hunched over, forearms propped on his thighs, hands knitted together. Out of the corner of my eye I could see his crosses dangling in front of him. There were three, of different sizes, and they twirled and twisted gently around each other. Guilt strung around his neck, for everyone to see. Mine was somewhere out in the water, but not gone from me. It would be mine for life.

"Nothing could be further from the truth, you know. About your mother."

For a second I wondered if I had spoken my thoughts aloud. He was looking at me with his sad eyes, so clear and present for someone I had first suspected might be crazy, but I reacted before I had a chance to think about it.

"The truth? I've always known the truth. I saw it. My mom walked out into the water one night when I was seven years old." I spat the words out, hard and angry. "She drowned herself. And all my life since then, everyone has called it an accident." I paused for a second, gathering my anger. "She left me on the beach that night, and it was no accident. She knew I was there, and you know what she did? She left me a piece of sea glass to find while she killed herself. *That's* the truth."

I looked down at my hands and drew in a shaky breath. The crawling man nodded, barely. Again, he seemed to be thinking.

"It was coming . . . long before you were around."

I looked up at him and ceased to breathe. "You knew my mom?"

He shook his head. "Knew of her. I've been here on this beach for a long time, and I've watched life go on all around it. And your mother, she was full of light, and life." He pursed his lips together and then spoke more carefully. "But she fought darkness too, some days. It was in her long before you came around. We all saw it." He was thinking back, looking at something I couldn't see.

"Did you live here? In one of the cottages?"

"Yes." He smiled, but his eyes remained sad. "The best days of my life I lived here. On the north side." We both glanced out the window. "That's where I would see her on the bad days, walking the beach alone, without your dad, and I knew on those days that she was fighting something nobody else understood."

I stared out at the water, remembering her good days and her bad ones, and he paused. Then he looked at me with purpose. "When you were born, you changed her. For the better. That's what children do."

My brain fired off questions in quick succession: *How could he know? He had seen us? What else had changed?*

He went on, and I listened so hard I forgot about the pain in my head and the ache in my limbs. "She would walk the beach with you, day and night, and a stranger could have seen how happy she was. It was like you were her whole world then, and that world must have become beautiful for her, because when I saw the two of you together, there was no trace of that darkness she'd had before."

He trailed off, then looked at me, almost reluctantly. "But it must have come back." The momentary lightness I had felt faded slowly at this, and I put my head down without speaking.

His voice was gentler now, and he spoke slowly, as if trying to ease me into what he was about to say. "Sometimes . . . a person is up against more than they can handle." He paused, long enough for me to wonder if he expected me to say something. But then he continued, and when he did, his voice quavered a bit. "And sometimes a person loses, no matter what they're fighting for."

I didn't understand what he meant. And I was frustrated. And tired. And now angry all over again. "Yeah?" I raised my eyebrows and my voice. "If I meant so much to her, she wouldn't have lost. If you're fighting for your whole world, how do you lose?"

The words hung heavy between us, and the crawling man didn't move. He drew in a shaky breath and let it out slowly before he spoke.

"I lost. I fought for my whole world, and I lost." He glanced down at the crosses, then back out at the water, and almost smiled. "I had a family once—a son, a daughter, and the love of my life." He bit his lower lip and nodded slowly before speaking again. "And I lost 'em out there, right in front of me."

My stomach went queasy. I flashed on the little boat. The kids' proud faces as they stood in front of it and their father, who still had the same clear eyes, though years and life had weighed them down.

I blinked once, twice, as if that would help me think of something to say.

"It wasn't your fault," I said softly. He looked up at me, and my voice gained confidence. "It's never been your fault. My dad has told that story to every lifeguard he's ever trained, and he's never once said it was your fault."

The crawling man looked at me steadily, and I went on.

"There was nothing you could have possibly done, possibly seen. . . . It wasn't your fault." I wanted to grab him by his wiry shoulders and make him understand, so he could stop. Instead I watched him stare out at the water for a long moment before he spoke.

He shook his head, ever so slightly. "They trusted me, and I couldn't save them."

I remembered the cracking sound my head had made when it had hit the rocks. The pain was still there, but dulled. I was too afraid to raise my hand to my head and feel the spot. The rest of my body, battered from being dragged over the rocks, ached and burned. And yet I was here.

"But you saved me. Today. On the rocks, in pounding surf, when there was no one else around and you could have drowned. You came from nowhere . . . and you saved me."

He looked up, and slowly it sunk in, enough to lighten his tired face just a bit.

"I guess . . . I guess I did."

27

The back door startled us both. "Hullo?" my dad's voice called. "Anna?" He was in the kitchen, setting down his gear, from the sound of it.

I cleared the emotion from my throat and brightened my voice as best I could. "In here." The Crawler looked at me with wide eyes, unsure what to do. I gave him a look meant to keep him quiet, just as my dad walked in carrying a take-out bag.

"Hey, hon. I got us some—" He looked from me to the Crawler, taking in our wet clothes and ragged appearance. "What—Is everything okay? What happened?" The concern in his voice made me feel instantly selfish and stupid for putting myself out there on the rocks. The what-ifs and possibilities would kill him. I struggled for an explanation.

The Crawler cleared his throat and squinted up at my dad. "Joseph, is it?"

My dad flinched slightly at this but recovered quickly and stuck his hand out, still trying to figure out what was going on. I kept quiet. "Uh . . . yes?"

The Crawler grasped his extended hand. "John Carter."

Recognition smacked my dad square in the face at the same time I saw in my mind the bunk beds and black-and-white pictures of a little boy and girl, tanned arms around each other's shoulders. And I understood why it had all been left there, just as it was.

"Mr. Carter. I—Wow. I had no idea it was you. . . . I thought you left . . . you left everything. . . .You just disappeared—"

John Carter nodded. "I did. For a while. But my life was here, and I . . . even with it all, I couldn't stay away." He inhaled deeply and looked at me. "Being here now, it's greater than the whole of the past." I felt my throat catch. My dad was silent. He had to be stunned that he hadn't recognized or guessed that it could be him. Or that he was sitting in our living room.

Mr. Carter smiled gently. "Seems we all find our way back here." He shifted his weight forward and put a hand on the coffee table to steady himself. "Also seems heroics run in your family." He motioned at me with a quick nod. "Your daughter here . . . she rescued me today. Banged herself up in the process too. You may want to take a look at the cut on her head."

Relief, and gratitude, and astonishment washed over me, and I tried not to show it as my dad eyed me, confused. His mouth opened to ask the first of many questions just as John Carter, the crawling man, pushed himself up and stood face-to-face with him, hand extended. I couldn't read my dad's thoughts, but I was sure we were struck by the same thing: He was standing.

My dad stepped forward and grasped his hand a second

time, then looked out at the falling rain. "Why don't you stay awhile? Until we get a break in the storm, at least. I can give you a ride home, make sure you're okay."

I eased myself up. "Yeah, we'll take you later."

He shook his head adamantly. "No, no. You've done enough. I will be fine." Then he looked back to my dad, serious. "It's your daughter who deserves your concern now. Stay with her." He said it in a way that somehow forced my dad not to argue.

He paused, thinking, instead. "Here, then. Take this, at least." He pulled off his jacket and handed it to Mr. Carter, who nodded and slid an arm into it.

"Thank you." Then he turned to me and leveled his eyes on mine. "And thank you, Anna. For more than you can understand. I only hope that one day someone can do the same for you."

He slid his eyes over to my dad, who wrapped an arm around my shoulder, and I looked down at a reddening bruise on the top of my foot, not sure of what to say. He had rescued me twice now, and I didn't have a way to thank him. Tears welled up again, and I bit the inside of my cheek, blinked them back, and nodded, hoping he knew.

My dad tried one last time. "You're sure we can't take you home?"

Mr. Carter held up his hand and shook his head with finality before he opened the door and stepped out into the rain. We watched as he raised his face to the sky, letting the drops hit his face, then walked away without looking back.

My dad turned to me, confused and bewildered. "What in the world was that about? What happened? Is your head okay?" He pulled my head toward him and inspected the cut, which had now stopped bleeding and had crusted over. "He was in the water? You helped him?"

I stood there and let him get all his questions out as I made up my mind. When the questions finally ran out, I sat back down in my chair and looked him square in the face, so nothing could be mistaken.

"Tell me the truth about Mom."

He had been winding up for another round of questions, still trying to figure out what had happened, but this caught him off guard and stopped him dead. He craned his neck forward and furrowed his brow, like he didn't understand what I meant. *"What?"*

I waited.

"I don't know what you mean," he fumbled. Clearly, though, he did, because he went chalk white and dead silent.

After what seemed like forever I broke the silence I had held on to for longer than anyone should. "I saw her that night, Dad. She left us. She left me, seven-year-old me, on the beach. And it wasn't an accident." My voice came out more tired than anything else, and I felt it. "She killed herself."

My dad swallowed hard and looked at the ground.

"And you knew," I said flatly. He blinked his eyes shut for a moment, then opened them right at me, and there was no trace of the lightness that sometimes danced there.

He sat down on the couch and ran a hand over his head before resting his elbows on his thighs. Then he looked at me again with heartbroken eyes. "Yeah. I knew it. But . . . I never knew how much you understood, so . . . I never . . . said it."

"For nine years?" I couldn't hide the sudden anger in my voice. "Do you have any idea what that's like?" The pain in my body and head were completely irrelevant now, and I stood up over him. "I saw her do it, Dad, and you said it was an accident, and so I went along with it, but I knew. And I was so scared that I knew, because I thought that if you found out, you would think it was all my fault." I took a breath and looked down, and when I spoke next, my voice was softer. "Because I was there. And she was upset with me." I didn't want to cry about it. It was so long ago.

He just sat there and looked at me. It was one of those moments when he probably should have pulled me in and hugged me, but it was there again, the space between us, and neither of us moved.

Finally he took a deep breath. "It wasn't your fault."

The same words I had said with such conviction to Jillian and to John Carter, but now they seemed hollow, and I knew better, because I remembered how it had been after she'd died. I spoke softly, knowing the strength of what I was about to say.

"But I thought it was. And *you* thought it was. That's why you couldn't even look at me for the longest time. I remember that, too." The words went right where I knew they would, and my dad sat, stricken, but I couldn't stop. "You wouldn't even look at me." Despite my valiant effort, I was crying.

He spoke slowly, in his voice that was reserved for grave matters.

"Anna. I couldn't look at you because every time I did, I was petrified—I couldn't imagine how I was going to do it alone." He looked down. "And because I thought, over and over, how she could have just as easily taken you out there with her. It killed me every time I let myself think it." By the look on his face, it still did. He shook his head. "No. I never, never blamed you. It took me a long time to stop blaming myself."

We were quiet then, and I turned the word over, again and again. "Blame." I had worn it around my neck for years. John Carter crawled under the weight of his. Jillian only set hers down when she ran. And nobody had ever told any of us we were to blame; we had just decided we were guilty. I sunk into my chair and looked over at my dad, who waited for me to say something, then I pulled the blanket tight around me and used the corner to wipe my eyes.

"How did you stop?" I sniffed. "Blaming yourself?"

Again he straightened up and took a deep breath, preparing. He looked at his hands briefly, then back at me. "Your mom was ill, Anna. I guess when I really accepted that, I stopped. I'm sure now they would call her depressed, or bipolar, or something else, but we didn't know then. We were young and stupid, and when we met, it was just beginning, I think." He smiled vaguely. "She was this wild, brave, brilliant girl who would do anything, and I fell for her the first time I saw her." I thought of him, a crazy-ass kid, kissing her in the moonlight, and I felt myself look at him with softer eyes. Of course he would want to remember her here, like that, and as he spoke, I did too.

"We spent two summers sneaking around here, hiding from her folks, and dreaming of running off together. Your grandparents were overprotective of her, and, looking back, they must have known she wasn't all right. There were times when she'd want to be alone, and I'd see her walking the beach, or she'd hole herself up and paint, but I never questioned it, because she'd always come back to me and we'd go right back to being happy and together. She was starting to fight it then, I think, but she hid it well." He scanned the water beyond the window, then looked back to me.

"You were born here, Anna, and she called you her little rescuer—" He stopped short, but then the thought came out in spite of his reluctance. "Said you'd saved her from the dark."

I said nothing. I barely breathed. A whole world I hadn't known about opened up in front of me, and I tried to make sense of my own history that changed and shifted as he spoke. I pictured her walking the beach with me, and John Carter and his kids watching from their porch in the warm afternoon sun. I pictured her telling me stories of mermaids and sea glass, and the magic of the water. And it was there, a connection between me and her, and this place. It was real.

"Why did we leave?"

My dad cleared his throat. "We left because I got hired on full-time right after you were born. I had to transfer to take the position, and that was hard on her. We got up there, and she tried to make the best of it, but it wore on her. I was having to work overtime to keep us afloat, and she was in a place that wasn't home to her, away from everything that was, and . . . she started to unravel . . . slowly." He paused, choosing his words carefully. "It was like she became two different people."

This felt familiar. This part I knew. The good days and the bad days.

"I should have seen it more clearly, I guess, but through everything else—work, money, life—I didn't. I kept thinking she'd get over it, or something would change, or it wasn't as bad as it seemed. . . ." He dropped his head, and I could see he hadn't completely let go of blaming himself. I struggled for the right thing to say, but before I could come up with it, he raised his eyes to mine.

"I've spent a lot of time wondering what I could have done differently, but I don't know if any of it would have worked. I don't know what was in her mind that night. I had to let that go, because she didn't leave me any answers or reasons." He pursed his lips together, and I could see that he was thinking something over. I waited. There had to be something more. The look on his face said there was.

"She didn't leave me with anything, but a while after . . . I found something that was meant for you." He hoisted himself up and disappeared into his room, and I fought the impulse to go with him. I had always wished she'd left me something, over and over had imagined a clue that would explain it all away or say it was all a dream, and that she was off somewhere beautiful, waiting for me.

My dad returned and held out to me a small unframed canvas. "I've been saving it . . . for the right time. It's the only painting of hers I kept."

I took it into my hands, almost afraid to look. And when I did, chills ran over me. It was a nighttime beachscape, and I recognized the tide pool rocks silhouetted in soft moonlight. The view from her window was calm, luminous, and spoke of gentle movement. I marveled at the care and detail, ran my fingers along the brushstrokes. And then I saw what I knew had to be there somewhere. Just outside of the moonlight's reflection, barely discernible, flicked a silvery tail, the curve of which hinted at the beauty that lay just below the surface.

I dropped my hands to my lap, the painting still in them, and stared out through the rain at the gray chop of the storm. My dad stepped closer, tentatively. "There's . . . something on the back." He sat down next to me and turned it over, and there, scrawled in the same graceful loops I'd seen in her room, was an inscription:

For Anna:
My Beauty, Grace, and Strength

Tears welled up in me again, and I looked up from the canvas to my dad, and I saw those things in him. I saw traces of grief and sadness that would always be there, but I also saw courage, and will, and goodness, all stemming from love at its purest. And so, without saying anything, I stepped over the space between us and put my arms around him, in an embrace that we hadn't ever had, past whatever barriers we had put up. We stayed that way for a long time, both of us with tears running warm down our faces, neither of us wanting to move.

He put his hand to the back of my head and must have felt the dried blood, because he pulled back and stood up to get a better look. "You did take a beating out there."

"Aah." I winced as he spread my hair to examine the cut. "I'm fine, I think, as long as you quit messing with it."

He peered down at it a moment longer, then looked at me intently. "Are you? Really?"

I let a breath out, and it took me a second, but I felt it. A lightness that hadn't been there before. She had left me something more. My fingers grazed the empty spot on my neck, and I glanced out the window before looking back at him. "I am." I nodded. "I'm okay. Are you?"

He thought for a second, then answered with a slow, tired smile. "Yeah. I am." It wasn't much. No big speech. No big talk. No elaborate scene. We had hugged. But something had shifted between us in that moment, and we both felt it. That didn't change the fact that my dad was a man of few words, or that he still wasn't quite sure what to do with a moment like that. He rubbed the top of my head. "Doesn't look like you'll be needing any stitches. . . ."

"Good."

"Surf is supposed to clean up by tomorrow. How 'bout we

get a morning session in and go for breakfast or something?"

"Um . . . school?"

He waved dismissively. "You can go late. I'll write you a note, or whatever."

I couldn't help but smile at his dadness as I nodded. "Okay. But I have to miss all of first period. It's Mr. Strickland."

He laughed. "Deal."

We sat for a while without saying much and watched the storm move over the water. It was barely dark and I hadn't eaten dinner, but exhaustion hung heavy over me. I stood up and stretched.

"I think I'm gonna go to bed. It's been way too long of a day."

My dad looked up. "You never told me what the deal was with Carter." He had scooted to the edge of the couch, ready to hear the story.

I shook my head. "It was nothing. . . . I'll tell you tomorrow. I'm too tired right now."

"All right." He smiled. "Get some sleep then."

I nodded and headed back to my room. I'd have some explaining to do to a few people tomorrow. Ashley and Jillian for sure. But I couldn't think of that now. Now I just needed quiet and rest.

In my bed, with my eyes closed, I ran my fingers over the bare spot on my neck and tried to distinguish between the sound of rain on the roof and the waves on the beach. Sleep closed in from the edges of my mind, and when I finally slipped into it, it was dreamless and deep.

28

The view out our front window looked like redemption. A line of pelicans glided low over the water and, though pale, the early morning sun silhouetted a wave as it crumbled lazily over the rocks and spilled up onto the sand. It carried on its back a surfer I took to be my dad. He rode it out with an ease that spoke of countless mornings spent in the water, then hopped off his board and scooped it up, looking back for a second before he turned his face to our window. And I saw it wasn't my dad at all. It was Tyler. I felt the zing as he waved.

"That Tyler out there?" My dad stepped in from the kitchen holding his cup of coffee.

"I think it is. Mind if I . . . ? I'll be right back." I grabbed a blanket from the couch and wrapped it around my shoulders, then near-ran down the stairs. When I got to the bottom, he was waiting, face still dripping wet, with his ever-present Tyler smile.

"Mornin', sunshine."

I felt myself break into a big, surprised, I-am-so-happy-to-see-you grin. "Hi." I almost laughed it instead of speaking it. "Um . . . do you usually surf out here before school and I just never noticed?"

"Nah." He set the end of his board in the sand and leaned an arm on it. "Usually Ab Point. But Ashley said you left the meet yesterday, and then you didn't answer the phone last night, so I thought I'd come by this morning. But it was early, and I didn't want to wake you up, so . . ." He looked me over just about the time I realized I was standing in my pajamas, my hair all tangled and matted, with a blanket wrapped around me. "You okay? Looks like you could've used a day at the spa with Ashley."

"Funny." I pulled the blanket tighter and reached a hand up to smooth my hair. "You have no idea . . ."

He took a step closer and smiled, and I felt his eyes run over me carefully, lingering a moment on the spot where I'd banged my head. "What happened yesterday?"

"That . . . is a really long story. But"—I took a step into him—"I'm okay. The storm's gone, I'm not going to first period, and here you are, first thing in the morning." I stood on my tiptoes and kissed the salt water from his lips. He took a small step back, and I had a feeling my dad was probably coming down the steps.

Tyler sighed. "You're leavin' me alone for Strickland's class, huh?"

"I know. Sorry to do it." I looked out over the water. "But look at it out there. It's a perfect morning—"

"Hey, Tyler."

Sure enough, Dad walked up and set his board on the sand, then reached around behind him to zip his wet suit. "Get some fun ones out there?"

"Yeah, it's good. Hard to leave it, but I can't miss first today." He looked over to me. "See you later?"

"Yeah. I'll find you," I said.

"All right. You guys have fun out there." He gave a quick nod, then tucked his board under his arm and jogged up the beach.

My dad kneeled over his board with a bar of wax, then stopped, smiling.

"What?" I fought the urge to smile too as I pulled the blanket up around my shoulders again. Heat crept up my cheeks.

He looked at me for a second, then shook his head. "Nothing. Just . . ." I opened my mouth for a rebuttal, but apparently, it wasn't needed. "Tyler's a good kid," he said. "He can come around whenever." He rubbed the wax on his board quickly, then stood up and motioned at the water. "Get suited up. I'll be out there."

"Okay. I'll be just a minute. There's something I need to do first."

He nodded, then grabbed his board and headed out. I stood there and watched him paddle out over the morning glass, so calm after such tumult, and when I turned to go up to the house, I thanked him silently, over and over, for being there.

This time, as I stood at the top of the sagging stairs in her little upstairs room, I felt her there with me. Out the framed window the exposed rocks covered in vibrant green moss stood out against the softness of the beach. The sand had been swept clean; no wood or glass, seaweed or bits of shells. The ocean had washed away everything, leaving behind a calm that spread out in me as I breathed it in. Beyond it all lay the expanse of the ocean, just beginning to sparkle beneath the rising sun as a new day unfurled itself. She'd captured it all perfectly in her frame, and in the pale morning light, it felt like peace.

I wrapped my quilt around me and ran my eyes over the painted window frame, thinking of the small canvas that now lay on my nightstand. Of the care and grace that she'd taken in her brushstrokes. For me. A brilliant artist, Joy had said. A side of my mother I never knew about, but the side she wanted me to know from the very beginning. And now, standing in the room that was once hers, looking out over the beach she once loved, it felt like I could.

A small, inside wave breaks, and cool water rushes up around my feet, carving out the sand beneath them as it recedes. I think of her then, and take another step into the water. And this time, as it swirls around my calves, I close my eyes and picture her as I want to remember her.

We walk the beach together, my little hand closed inside of hers. We are looking for treasures— pieces of glass, broken upon the beach, then smoothed over into more beautiful, softer versions of themselves, gem-like in their beauty. She tells me how the very best ones have been tossed beneath the waves so long they no longer have any sharp edges. I nod seriously, but inside think of how I'd one day like to see the center of one of those smooth pieces, where it's still clear and pure, because even the ocean can't shape that.

When I open my eyes, I look down instinctively, and it's there, beside my foot. She's returned it to me. I kneel down and reach with my free hand, through the water just in time to grasp my piece of moonglass before the white water wipes the slate clean. When I hold it up in the morning sun, I can see it has cracked wide open. Split where a hole had been drilled for the chain. And inside it's the truest, most beautiful red I've ever seen.